PILLOW TALK CONSCIOUSNESS

Intimate Reflections on America's
100 Most Interesting
Thoughts and Suspicions

ALSO BY

ERVIN (EARL) COBB
AND
CHARLOTTE D. GRANT-COBB, PHD

BOOKS

Living a Richer Life
Getting the Most out of Life's Gifts and Circumstances

Focused Leadership
A 10-Step Approach to Leading and Winning When it Matters

Navigating the Life Enrichment Model™

Until I Change

Transition

VIDEO PROGRAMS

Get Ready to Reap All the Richness Your Life Has to Offer

All of the above are available at your local bookstore or may be ordered by visiting:
www.richerlifeassociates.com

PILLOW TALK CONSCIOUSNESS

Intimate Reflections on America's 100 Most Interesting Thoughts and Suspicions

Ervin (Earl) Cobb
Charlotte D. Grant-Cobb, PhD

‡RICHER Publications
An Imprint of Richer Life, LLC

Published by ⫽RICHER Publications
An Imprint of Richer Life, LLC

4600 E. Washington Street, Suite 300, Phoenix, Arizona 85034
www.richerlifeassociates.com

Cover Design: Richer Media USA • Photographs: Big Stock Photo

Paul and Paulette are "fictitious characters".

Library of Congress Cataloging-in-Publications Data

Pillow Talk Consciousness: Intimate Reflections on
America's 100 Most Interesting Thoughts and Suspicions
Ervin (Earl) Cobb and Charlotte D. Grant-Cobb -- 1st edition
p.   cm.

1. Psychology   2. Relationships   3. Reference
ISBN 978-0-9744617-4-8 (pbk : alk. Paper)

ISBN 13: 978-0-9744617-4-8

ISBN 10: 0-9744617-4-8

Text set is Adobe Garamond

PRINTED IN THE UNITED STATES OF AMERICA

First edition

A C E G I K J H F D B

ACKNOWLEDGMENTS

Thanks to the colleagues and friends who volunteered to collaboratively share their thoughts, insights and wisdom to improve this book.

CONTENTS

"And we're seeing a higher level of consciousness and many more opportunities for people to challenge their present ways of thinking and move into a grander and larger experience of who they really are."

Neale Donald Walsch

PROLOGUE

"Life is a state of consciousness." Emmet Fox

A Pillow Talk *State of Being*

This year will mark 30 years of us being together as a couple. As we reflect back on the approximately 10,950 days and nights, we are proud of the fact that there were only a few of those nights that we have not gone to bed together. Some of the most memorable discussions we have had over this period have usually occurred late at night as we were about to fall asleep and when one of us would say …"honey" or "sweetheart", let me tell you what happened today.

One evening a few years ago, prior to falling off to sleep, we began a conversation regarding how much we both looked forward to having the opportunity to share some of the thoughts that had surfaced and stayed with us during the day. We laughed at the idea that most of the things we shared, during what is supposed to be the most intimate time of the day, had nothing to do with romance.

We observed that the things we shared were usually thoughts and suspicions surrounding people, problems, politics, perceptions, philosophy and personal passions. Many were based on comments from co-workers or discussions we had with family and friends. Some had their genesis from television and radio pundits or from an article we had read in a newspaper.

While expressing our opinion on a specific topic, we would sometimes surprise each other with uncommon frankness and perplexing points-of-view.

Some of the most interesting thoughts seemed to have silently penetrated our subconscious during the day and unexpectedly surfaced just as sleep was about to render one of us comatose. At times it appeared that some of the comments were not worthy of sharing. Nevertheless, we both valued the intimacy and the insightfulness of these unscripted and precious moments of interchange.

As we further examined this nightly ritual, we began to realize that for some strange reason, during these moments of unusual *"pillow talk"*, we both seemed to transcend our typical dose of human consciousness. We would find ourselves in a *"state of being"* which momentarily provided an elevated level from which we could express and openly share our subjective awareness of the world around us, our perceptions, our true feelings and our internal thoughts.

We initially attributed this state of being to the fact that we loved and trusted each other. We also felt that the comfort of being locked in the security and serenity of our own home was a contributing factor.

However, in the back of our minds, we suspected that something cognitive and more profound was at play. These intimate and revealing interchanges seemed to be propelled by the energy we were generating as a result of being wrapped in this elevated level of consciousness.

Following this initial conversation, our curiosity peaked regarding the states of consciousness and the inherent significance that can be associated with *pillow talk* as a powerful form of human expression. Over the next several months we continued our pursuit for and research of, at least, a rudimentary understanding of this phenomenon that we, at this point, were calling a *pillow talk state of being.*

Individualism and a Pureness of Thought

During our pursuit for more clarity surrounding our somewhat unusual *pillow talk*, we reflected on many of our late night conversations. We realized that while we were in this *pillow talk state of being* we would, without hesitation, open up to each other as two human beings rather than being channeled by the protocols typically linked to conversation between *man and woman, husband and wife* or *life partners*.

Our behavior and anxious desire to share and respond to each other with candor would appear to be almost childlike. Furthermore, it seemed that we both expressed our thoughts in a manner that was unchecked by the normal level of societal restraint and mindfulness.

At this point, our primary objective was to find the answer to the questions, *"What was the catalyst for generating such a high level of consciousness during these peculiar pillow talk moments and why we behaved the way we did?"* As a consequence of our efforts, we were drawn to the research we performed several years earlier while writing our last book, *Living a Richer Life: Getting the Most out of Life's Gifts and Circumstances*.

We recalled that we had discovered several interesting revelations regarding the significant role that *human behaviors* and *societal influences* play in shaping what we all think, how we all think and, to some degree, our ability to openly share our thoughts with others. Mainstream to this research is an idea that is expressed in a Buddha quote which states, *"We are shaped by our thoughts; we become what we think. When the mind is pure, joy follows like a shadow that never leaves."*

Also relevant to this point-of-view are the insights we had acquired from Paul R. Lawrence, Professor of Organizational

13

Behavior at Harvard Business School and Nitin Nohria, Dean of Harvard Business School and previously Head of the Organizational Behavior Unit. In their book, *Driven: How Human Nature Shapes Our Choices,* the professors discuss the four basic motivations that they believe can be used to explain almost all of human behavior.

According to their research, although we all believe that we are unique and individuals, we are also arguably more similar than we are different from one another.

Our common needs and desires (or "drives" as they call them) are as much the product of evolutionary processes as are "the physical characteristics of Galapagos finches."[2] Thus, these "drives" are common to all humans in all cultures. The four drives are designated as follows:

- *"The drive to acquire objects and experiences that improve our status relative to others;*
- *The drive to establish long-term bonds with others based on reciprocity;*
- *The drive to learn about and make sense of our world, which is largely our own social creation; and*
- *The drive to defend ourselves, our families and friends, our beliefs and our resources."*[2]

We saw an opportunity here to perhaps build a case that the elevated level of consciousness associated with a *pillow talk state of being* was simply driven by a natural and humanistic need to make sense of our world. In addition, maybe it is the love that two people have for each other and the security of their own home that help to expedite an escape from the typical daily chatter between husband and wife.

However, some of the most important lessons we learned from our research while writing *Living a Richer Life* are all grounded in the unsuspecting affects that societal influence has on almost every aspect of our lives, including the bedroom.

Social influence occurs when our individual thoughts, feelings or actions are affected, negatively or positively, by other people --- including family members, friends, neighbors and co-workers.

The three major influences in America, as in most societies, are political influences, economic influences and cultural influences. The political influences consist of the local, state and federal governments and the laws and regulations set by the governing parties. Economic influences encompass the rate of employment, gross domestic product, incidence of poverty and the structure of economic activity. The cultural influences consist of the institutions and voluntary associations of our society such as the churches, media, education systems along with the influence of national figures and celebrities.

Perhaps the combination of the need to escape the negative effects of societal influences and human behavior could also build a case in support of the elevated level of consciousness associated with *pillow talk* moments.

But, the reality is that we are all individuals capable of taking control of almost every aspect of our lives based on our will, determination and spirit. In the words of Oscar Wilde *"Society exists only as a mental concept; in the real world there are only individuals."*

Thus, we have come to believe that what we experience as we are wrapped in the comfort of a *pillow talk state of being* is in all likelihood an elevated sense of individualism and humanity combined with the inherent freedoms which accompany intimacy and security. Through this individualism, we can promote independence and self-reliance. Our individualism empowers a natural desire to oppose most external interference upon our own interests, whether by society, family or any other group or institution.

Through our humanity, intimacy and feeling of security, we recognize the frailties of humans and embrace the trust of a loved one to protect us in our most transparent state of being --- thus, enabling an elevated level of *consciousness* and a *pureness of thought*.

Levels of Consciousness

The consciousness we all operate in is actually equivalent to the mental, spiritual and psychological lens we use to see reality. The perceptions, beliefs, mindsets and values you hold right now are a result of the consciousness you are operating in.

Whenever any of us experience a shift in our consciousness due to an inner realization [such as a *pillow talk state of being*], we are, even if only momentarily, actually transcending our normal level of consciousness. As a result, we transcend or rise above our normal belief systems, fears and attitudes. This is the same as detaching the old or normal set of lenses we used to see reality and replacing them with new ones.

As mentioned above, consciousness is like the lens you use to view your reality. Being at a different or elevated level of consciousness means you are using a different lens to view the world. Your thoughts, feelings, beliefs, values and actions are outputs of the level of consciousness at which you operate.

While the object you are observing (i.e. life, the world, events in your life, yourself, your spouse, your partner) can remain the same, just having or operating at an elevated level of consciousness causes the way you see them to be widely different.

Let's take "nearsightedness" as an analogy. The normal result of nearsightedness presents what you see, with the lowest level of correction, as a blurred image. In this analogy, when you focus on yourself at the lowest level, you can't see anything beyond an extremely distorted sense of your self-worth and your world. At a higher level of correction, however, that visual fog lifts and you develop higher clarity of yourself, the world and your place in the world. Your vision becomes less hazy and more accurate. The higher the level of correction, the higher the clarity and your vision of what the world around you entails.

All these changes come from just a change in your consciousness. However, in reality, nothing about life or the world around you has changed. To increase your consciousness level thus translates into a more accurate viewpoint of reality.

Based on the enormity of the ecstasy we both experienced while wrapped in the comfort of a *pillow talk state of being*, we were certain, as our research confirmed, consciousness is at the heart of all of our existence. However, we also learned that most experts in the field find it hard to talk about consciousness without perplexing language which may include Darwinian, mystical, metaphysical, philosophical and psychological.

Consciousness poses one of the most baffling challenges in the "science of the mind" today. There is nothing that we know more intimately than conscious experience, but there is nothing that is harder to explain. All sorts of mental phenomena have yielded to scientific investigation in recent years, but consciousness has stubbornly resisted. Many have tried to explain it, but the explanations always seem to fall short of the mark.

But, most experts do agree that life requires us to be conscious. They also agree that we must use our consciousness to function in the world and the notion of levels of consciousness has been with us for some time.

Pillow Talk Consciousness

Whereas Science itself seems perplexed when it has to address questions regarding consciousness, we have concluded the following:

- The notion of a *pillow talk state of being* is plausible, powerful and positive. The elevated level of consciousness experienced during these times is tangible, peculiar and best referred to as a state of *Pillow Talk Consciousness* --- a powerful form of human expression; and

- We are almost certain that we *are not* the only couple [over the history of mankind] who has enjoyed these intimate, insightful dialogues.

Being the inquisitive authors and Americans that we are, we were naturally driven to ask ourselves…if we were flies on the wall of the average household experiencing the wonder of *pillow talk consciousness*, what would be the tenor and the composition of the most interesting thoughts and suspicions?

Consequently, we spent much of the past year researching and identifying what we believe to be the 100 most common topics that frame the *lives* and *conversations* of average American households thus far in the 21st Century. We based our selection on current events, news headlines, national polling, etc. Then, we began to research and construct "one" *probable dialogue* for each topic.

The dialogues have been constructed to be brief, candid and thought-provoking. Each dialogue contains a set of what might be considered our nation's most intriguing thoughts and suspicions at this nexus of the 21st century.

Since each American is the product of the sum of their biological heritage, environment, teachings, beliefs and other factors which define their individualism, there are conceivably as many unique *probable dialogues* as there are American households.

Therefore, for *Pillow Talk Consciousness: Intimate Reflections on American's 100 Most Interesting Thoughts and Suspicions,* we created the archetypal characters and voices of Paul and Paulette to serve the role of an early 21st century American couple. Each of the dialogues presented has been created to embody how we believe the biological heritage, environment, teachings and beliefs of these "fictitious characters" might shape their comments, questions and responses.

It is our hope that as you get to know Paul and Paulette and become entwined in their frank and unrestrained *pillow talk*, you will be able to associate the tenor and the composition of their dialogues with their character and personality. As in real life, we are all influenced by our life experiences --- including our personality, family, friends, life style, occupation, educational background, social status, politics and religious affiliation.

Hopefully, you will feel compelled to make note of *your point of view* in the book [an area is provided] and log your own thoughts and suspicions vis-à-vis each topic. Perhaps by sharing this book, including your own annotations, with others (i.e. family

PILLOW TALK CONSCIOUSNESS

members, friends, neighbors and classmates) you will be rewarded with some stimulating and informative dialogues of your own.

Regardless of how you choose to read or use this book, we trust that you will find *Pillow Talk Consciousness* an insightful, engaging, unique and thought-provoking experience.

Ervin (Earl) Cobb
Charlotte D. Grant-Cobb, PhD
Phoenix, Arizona

II. Paul

"Life is a series of sensations connected to different states of consciousness."

Remy de Gourmont

Paul

When asked, "What is your favorite ice cream?" Paul looks up and answers, "Whatever Paulette has in the refrigerator."

Paul Sigmund Schuhmacher, Jr. was born shortly before midnight on February 3, 1948 in the suburbs of Chicago, Illinois. His family moved from Chicago to Minnesota when he was eight years old. He was raised in New Ulm, Minnesota where he grew up to be a burly yet quite handsome young man. New Ulm is known as the City of "Charm and Tradition". The small town is nestled just 90 miles southwest of the Twin Cities, in the heart of the scenic Minnesota River Valley.

Paul was the oldest of three children born to Paul Sr. and his mother Patricia, who was affectionately called Patty. His parents were devout Catholics and consciously passed down their faith to Paul and his two brothers, Patrick and Peter.

Paul Sr. and Patty were German immigrants. Their move to New Ulm in 1956 was well planned. Paul Sr. had always wanted to raise his sons with a real sense of their German heritage. The small town of New Ulm was founded in 1854 by German immigrants and named after the city of Ulm in southern Germany. The population of New Ulm in the early 1950's was only around 8,700. Approximately 98% of the town's inhabitants were of Eastern-European descent. The town was also rich in German culture. New Ulm regularly celebrated its German heritage with festivals featuring traditional music, food and beer.

Patty was the musician of the Schuhmacher family. She had mastered the piano and the organ at an early age. Patty performed during many of New Ulm's festive community events. She also devotedly provided lessons to all three of her sons from the time they were three years old. Only Paul Jr. seemed to take a real liking to music. By the age of twelve, he had become quite accomplished in his own right.

Paul Sr. was, without question, the leader of the household. He owned a hardware store located in the town square and a small woodworking business. He was a descendant of generations of skilled craftsmen. He was also determined that his sons develop their gifts of German craftsmanship.

From the time Paul Jr., Patrick and Peter were walking age, they could be found at the family store late in the afternoon helping their father with small tasks. Paul Sr. would insist that they watch him closely as he performed various crafts around the store. He would then quiz them after supper regarding any new techniques he had used that day.

All three sons respected and appreciated their father. They felt the need to perfect all of the woodworking tasks they were given in order to please him.

As Paul Jr. grew older, his behavioral and physical features were almost identical to his father. However, he was always a mother's boy. His mother was a stay at home mom. Things stayed that way until the youngest son, Peter, went away to college. After arriving in the United States in the 1920's, Patty was the impetus behind the push for her and Paul Sr. to become naturalized citizens as quickly as possible.

When Patty and Paul Sr. first discussed the idea of leaving the Chicago area, she really wanted to move east to New York or Maine. However, following the move to Minnesota, she quickly assumed all of the stereotypical Midwestern qualities. Many of which were innate to her German heritage.

She raised her sons with a strong work ethic. She made sure that they understood that they had a couch, not a sofa. She asked them to take out the garbage, not the trash. On Saturday afternoons, when the boys were young, she would take them to town to purchase pop, not soda, and bring them home in a bag and not a sack.

Paul Jr. most admired his mother's determination and her strength. To him, she was the epitome of self-assurance. This was a trait that Paul Jr. not only admired but inherited.

Paul Jr. was an excellent student in school. He graduated top of his class from the Cathedral High School in New Ulm. The family struggled with whether to keep the boys in the New Ulm Area Catholic School System or to allow them to attend the New Ulm Public High School to gain a better sense of cultural diversity. By the early 1960's, New Ulm's population had grown to over 11,000 and included new arrivals with more ethnically and culturally diverse backgrounds. However, the change in schools was never more than talk and all of the Schuhmacher boys graduated from Cathedral High.

Being a good student served Paul Jr. well during his early adulthood and beyond. He was accepted into Minnesota State University at Mankato. Mankato was located 75 miles southwest of Minneapolis-St. Paul. In 1966, MSU had the third largest student body in the state of Minnesota with over 15,000 students. Paul received a full four-year scholarship as a part of the Maverick Army ROTC Program. He majored in Electrical Engineering with a minor in music. He lettered as a member of both the ice hockey and swim teams.

Paul graduated in 1970 with honors. He accepted a commission as a Second Lieutenant in the United States Army. After four years of active duty, which included a yearlong tour in Vietnam, he was allowed to join the Army Reserve to fulfill the remainder of his eight-year military commitment.

Paul was hired by an Information Systems Company in 1975 as a systems engineer. It was on a business trip that same year to New York when he first met Paulette. He was introduced to her by a friend. Later that evening he met her for dinner in a small German-American restaurant in Manhattan. She was working in New York as a financial analyst for a Wall Street investment firm. She quickly shared that she was only a year out of a bad marriage. It was a marriage that lasted only three years. There were no children, but plenty of blame.

Paulette and Paul's personalities and interests seemed to be a perfect match. Paulette saw Paul Jr. as smart and athletic but with a gentle and inquisitive personality. Paul admired Paulette's strong mind, financial savvy, vivid imagination and rather shapely, trim body.

Paul and Paulette dated for a little over a year. Paulette insisted that she spend all four seasons with him prior to making any long term commitments. They were married in Burlington, Vermont on July 4, 1977. They both soon settled in Minneapolis. It was not long before they purchased their first and only home.

Paul became a senior, highly touted and well-respected technologist. Paulette transitioned into community banking and became a regional vice president. They raised two children within whom they instilled their German and Midwestern values.

On July 4, 2011, the Schuhmachers celebrated 34 years of marriage. Their son, David, turned twenty-nine years old in April and finally married his longtime girlfriend, Jeanette, in June of that year. Their twenty-six year old daughter Josie graduated with a nursing degree from San Francisco State University in 2009. Josie and her partner Janet were into their fifth year of enjoying San Francisco and each other.

"No problem can be solved from the same level of consciousness that created it."

Albert Einstein

III. Paulette

"When you change the way you look at things, the things you look at change."

Wayne W. Dyer

Paulette

When asked, "How would you like to start your dream vacation?" Paulette smiles and says, "By getting off the airplane alone."

Paulette Lisa McClain-Schuhmacher was born on September 9, 1951 in Burlington, Vermont. Historic Burlington, on Lake Champlain, is a great place to grow up if you can handle the wind off the Lake. Both of her parents grew up in Vermont. Paulette's mother, Carol, was from Brattleboro and her father, Raymond (Ray), was born and raised in Burlington. Her parents

31

met while attending the University of Vermont. Paulette's father worked as an electrical engineer at a large aerospace facility in Burlington until retirement. Her mother, Carol (nee Anderson), worked as a middle-school math teacher and doubled as the art teacher as well as a yearbook advisor.

Ray and Carol had three daughters, Lillie, Margaret and Paulette. Paulette was the youngest of the three. The McClains were devout Catholics and all of the girls practiced catechism at Cathedral of the Immaculate Conception.

Ray and Carol insisted that their girls stay focused on their school-work, but they also liked to have fun with their children. Family outings included picnics, boating and, of course, hockey. Paulette was the family athlete. She excelled in ice skating and gymnastics. Her lifelong love for exercise and fitness would contribute to her ability to maintain her shapely figure.

Ray raised his daughters to believe they could obtain anything that they dreamed. He completed college when only a handful of women participated in the then male-dominated engineering field. He strived to be a champion for equal opportunity and was supportive of all the women with whom he worked. Although Ray was serious about his career, he never took himself too seriously. To his family and friends, Ray was the quintessential "Vermonter," – hardy and forbearing – with a "Vermonter's sense of humor."

Carol was equally proud of her Brattleboro roots. She considered it an honor to be the keeper of the Estey organ that had been in her family for years. Carol learned to play the organ on that Estey and she instilled in her girls a love of both music and math.

Growing up in the McClain household was a little chaotic because the McClain girls were active in everything. In addition to Paulette's ice skating and gymnastics, Margaret was active in drama and Lillie was a concert-level pianist. Nevertheless, Ray and Carol ran a tight ship --- grades first, then extracurricular activities.

Ray usually picked up Paulette from the rink or gym while Carol patiently balanced piano lessons and rehearsals after school. Between ice skating, gymnastics and school, Paulette had little time for "fun" high school events like dances and bonfires.

Ray and Carol first spotted Paulette's natural math skills when she was in the 5th grade. They nurtured her love of math. In fact, all of the McClain girls were competent in math. Margaret and Lillie both chose careers as high school math teachers. For a long while, everyone thought Paulette would become an engineer like Ray, but math formulas won her heart.

Paulette graduated from high school in 1968 and was awarded a full scholarship to the University of Vermont. It was not a surprise that she majored in math. Paulette rebelled from the discipline and rigors of athletics when she entered U of V and met Michael Knox, a fellow math major. Paulette did not believe that she could actually meet someone who enjoyed math as much as she did.

Paulette and Michael dated through their undergraduate years and were married shortly before moving to New York after accepting jobs on Wall Street. Paulette's position was as a financial analyst and Michael accepted a position as a quantitative analyst. Michael missed the "purity" of math, as he called it, and decided to pursue a graduate degree at City University in New York while maintaining his quantitative analyst position. The young marriage could not handle the strain of school and work.

Michael and Paulette found themselves separated in less than a year and finally divorced after only three years of marriage. Since this was the first real "failure" for both of them, neither of them handled the divorce very well. There was plenty of blame to go around.

Paulette blamed Michael for taking on too much, neglecting her and not being sensitive to her needs. Michael blamed Paulette for not being more considerate of his career goals and of even being too selfish. Paulette's parents felt that their baby married too soon. They only hoped the experience would not discourage her from seeking a happy marriage and would serve as an unfortunate, but valuable, character building episode in her young life.

Paulette was still a little raw a year after the divorce when she was introduced to an interesting young man named Paul Schuhmacher by a colleague during a gathering after work. Not expecting anything to come of it, she met Paul later that evening for dinner at a favorite restaurant in Manhattan. They liked each other right way.

Paul was a Vietnam veteran and an engineer, like her Dad. He turned out to be a truly nice guy. He was attractive, with a military polish that implied discipline, athleticism and strength. He had a gentle spirit and inquisitive personality. Paul also turned out to be truly interested in Paulette. He bombarded her with questions regarding what she did and what she liked.

Paulette and Paul dated for a little over a year. From her first marriage, Paulette had learned that you could spend a lot of time with someone and still not really get to know them at all. But, she was not ready to fall in love without knowing Paul through, at least, four seasons.

All doubts were removed when she introduced Paul to the McClain family. First, Paul loved hockey like a "Vermonter," and second, he shared her Dad's quirky sense of humor. Of course, Ray couldn't let it be known that he liked Paul right away. Paulette knew Paul was welcome in the family when Ray started teasing Paul by telling him a Minnesotan could never make it through a Vermont winter. It also didn't hurt that Paul had minored in music and was Catholic. Carol, Margaret and Lillie were impressed. Despite the fact that the marriage would take Paulette even further away, Paul was welcomed into the family.

Paulette and Paul were married in Burlington at the Cathedral of the Immaculate Conception on July 4, 1977, with the fireworks on Lake Champlain as a backdrop. Paulette's financial acumen was valued immediately by a community bank in Minnesota. Several mergers and acquisitions gave that Minnesota bank an instant, national presence and Paulette soon moved into a senior management position as a Regional Vice President. Paul emerged as a valued senior technologist with the multinational computer company he joined in 1975 after leaving the military.

Carol and Lillie were in Minnesota with Paul's mother, Patty, when Paulette gave birth to their first child, David. All the McClains joined all of the Schuhmachers for the birth of their daughter, Josie, about three years later.

The four seasons had grown into over 140 seasons by the time they celebrated their 34th wedding anniversary on July 4, 2011. Paulette was delighted to have the opportunity to plan the marriage ceremony for David and his longtime girlfriend, Jeanette. David pursued engineering like his Dad while Josie went into nursing. David remained in Minnesota, while Josie stayed in San Francisco after earning her degree from San Francisco State University.

"The key to growth is the introduction of higher dimensions of consciousness into our awareness."

Lao Tzu

IV. America's 100 Most Interesting Thoughts and Suspicions

Topics that Frame the Lives and Conversations of Average Americans in the 21st Century

1. Abortion
2. Aging
3. Air Travel
4. Art
5. Automobiles
6. Banking
7. Bullying
8. Capitalism
9. Careers
10. Celebrity
11. Choices
12. Children
13. Church
14. Citizenship
15. College
16. Competition
17. Computers
18. Conservative
19. Corporations
20. Death
21. Democracy
22. Dieting
23. Drug Wars
24. Education
25. Entertainment
26. Entitlements
27. Entrepreneurship
28. Exercise
29. Failure
30. Faith
31. Family
32. Family Values
33. Fatherhood
34. Financial Security
35. Food
36. Free Enterprise
37. Friendship
38. Funerals
39. Gender
40. Government
41. Group Think
42. Guns
43. Health
44. Healthcare
45. Home Foreclosure
46. Homosexuality
47. Illegal Drugs
48. Immigration
49. International Affairs
50. Internet
51. Insurance
52. Intelligence
53. Jobs
54. Labor Unions
55. Legacy
56. Liberal
57. Life
58. Love
59. Marriage
60. Media
61. Men
62. Military
63. Mortgages
64. Motherhood
65. Motivation
66. Music
67. Obesity
68. Parenting
69. Philanthropy
70. Politics
71. Poverty
72. Prayer
73. Prejudice
74. Prescription Drugs
75. Prison
76. Privilege
77. Real Estate
78. Reality Shows
79. Relationships
80. Religion
81. School
82. Security
83. Self Awareness
84. Sex
85. Social Media
86. Socialism
87. Social Security
88. Society
89. Sports
90. Stock Market
91. Stupidity
92. Success
93. Taxes
94. Technology
95. Travel
96. Voting
97. War
98. Weather
99. Women
100. Work Ethic

ABORTION

Paulette: Sweetheart. Did you realize it has been over 38 years since Roe v Wade struck down state laws banning abortion?

Yet, the political discussion and controversy surrounding the moral and legal status of abortion continues.

Paul: No. I didn't realize that it has been almost forty years. Time really flies.

Paulette: I have never shared this with you…but, I have always felt that women could take the abortion issue off the political table, if they wished.

I wonder if men got pregnant instead of women, would they demand the legal right to choose.

Paul: Now, Paulette. Why would you even think of such a ridiculous thing?

Paulette: Ridiculous? You mean men getting pregnant or men not wanting the right to choose?

Paul: Both.

YOUR POINT OF VIEW?

_____
_____
_____
_____
_____
_____
_____
_____
_____
_____
_____
_____
_____
_____
_____
_____
_____
_____
_____
_____
_____
_____
_____

AGING

Paul: Paulette, are you awake?

Paulette: Yes, I am Dear.

Paul: I was flipping through an AARP magazine today and noticed a very interesting statistic.

Paulette: Really…what was so interesting?

Paul: Well…according to the latest census, a quarter of the U.S. population is under 20 years of age and people our age comprise only one-eighth of the population. I wonder what this means in terms of America's future.

Paulette: It depends on whether or not those 18 years and older register and actually vote in every election.

Paul: And if they do not?

Paulette: We older people will continue to dominate the ballet box while looking through our bifocals and the rear-view mirror. We just can't get beyond being swayed by the politics of gun rights, abortion, gay marriage, race relations and family values. That's how the powerful and upper class in our society continue to preserve elite educations for their kids and deprive the vast majority of everyone else's kids from obtaining their fair share of the American dream.

Paul: Of course…maturity, birth rights and elections do matter.

YOUR POINT OF VIEW?

_____

_____

_____

_____

_____

_____

_____

_____

_____

_____

_____

_____

_____

_____

_____

_____

_____

_____

_____

_____

_____

_____

_____

_____

AIR TRAVEL

Paul: Sweetheart. Do you remember meeting Larry Dean, my logistics manager, during last years' Holiday party?

Paulette: Yes. I do remember meeting Larry and his wife Selma.

Paul: At work today Larry shared with me that a male TSA agent fondled him during a body search in the Atlanta airport. He is considering filing legal action and not flying that airline ever again.

Paulette: Paul. Larry is five-feet tall and must weight over 350 pounds. Now…why would anyone want to intentionally fondle someone like Larry?

Paul: You just don't know what to expect from commercial air travel these days. I hear that this particular airline is in financial trouble and considering filing for bankruptcy…again. I suspect that they are attempting to discourage overweight people from flying, so that they can save on fuel cost.

Paulette: Well, that would be a creative way for the airlines to expedite more bankruptcies, consolidations and lawsuits. With the reality of rising fuel cost, risky offshore maintenance and subsidized ticket pricing, the airline industry could be the next "financial bubble" soaring over the U.S. economy. As those responsible for oversight…see no evil and hear no evil…again.

YOUR POINT OF VIEW?

ART

Paul: It's bedtime...what are you reading, Honey?

Paulette: An interesting article on America's Great Depression of the 1930's. The writers are comparing that major economic downturn with the current downturn, which is being called the Great Recession of 2008/2009.

You know...I didn't realize that the Great Depression lasted as long as it did.

Paul: I believe it started in 1929 with the Stock Market crash and didn't end until 1941 with America's entry into World War II.

Paulette: That's correct...over twelve years. According to this article, after the Great Depression hit, President Roosevelt's New Deal of the 1930's created Public Arts programs to give work to artists and decorate public buildings, usually with a "national theme".

Do you think what's being called the Great Recession of 2008/2009 will "target" the Arts?

Paul: Yes. Absolutely.

Paulette: Do you mean leading to more Public Arts programs?

Paul: No. Art is being targeted for elimination by those who equate anything even remotely associated to a "national theme" to big government and higher taxes.

Paulette: But, art is the expression of a caring nation's creativity and imagination.

Paul: I rest my case.

PILLOW TALK CONSCIOUSNESS

YOUR POINT OF VIEW?

AUTOMOBILES

Paulette: I read today that the U.S. Strategic Oil Reserve would maintain our automotive life style for only about 80 days.

Paul: That's hard to believe. Over the last 100 years America has perfected the mass production of automobiles; built the world's biggest oil companies; modernized and globalized communications; created the largest corporations in the world and deregulated a massive U.S. banking system.

How do we go about determining why we are still trapped in automobiles fueled with gasoline?

Paulette: Well…maybe we should start with the automobile, oil, communications, corporate and banking lobbies.

Paul: I do not believe that they are that powerful and selfish.

Paulette: As I recall, history has shown that it is easier for most of us to accept incremental change from positions of power. The risk of upsetting the status quo and loosing privilege with such a revolutionary change as not profiting from "gasoline engines" and "increasing gas prices" seems to be humanly unbearable.

Paul: I see your point…and selfishness is a human quality sometimes disguised as special interest and capitalism.

YOUR POINT OF VIEW?

_____
_____
_____
_____
_____
_____
_____
_____
_____
_____
_____
_____
_____
_____
_____
_____
_____
_____
_____
_____
_____
_____

BANKING

Paulette: This is almost unbelievable and scary.

Paul: What's that Sweetheart?

Paulette: I read today that two years since the banking system nearly imploded, requiring a massive government bailout, the U.S. currently has almost 8,000 active banks with over 13 trillion dollars in assets. The five biggest banks have now repaid government bailout funds, raised billions of dollars to strengthen capital ratios and their stock prices are trading three to four times higher. However, the majority of Americans lack confidence in the stability of the U.S. banking system. This is so scary.

Paul: I know. What a mess. We are educated people and it scares us to death. How did these institutions that were set up to simply be a place where money changes hands become uncontrollable financial giants and "too big to fail"?

Paulette: Good question. Unfortunately, most Americans also do not have a clue. We all seemed to have just awakened one morning to find an unprecedented level of home foreclosures, long-term unemployment and uncertain futures waiting for us. Unlike most previous U.S. domestic crises, this one really requires a combined ethical, financial and humanitarian approach to an equitable solution.

Paul: I think you're right…but such a solution is very difficult to achieve…especially in the polarized, lobbyist-driven political environment we have today in this country.

YOUR POINT OF VIEW?

_____

_____

_____

_____

_____

_____

_____

_____

_____

_____

_____

_____

_____

_____

_____

_____

_____

_____

_____

_____

_____

_____

_____

BULLYING

Paulette: Paul. Are you asleep?

Paul: Not any more…what's up?

Paulette: I must share something with you. I had lunch with my new manager, Doris, today. I was shocked to hear how much energy she and her husband are putting into dealing with the issue of bullying surrounding their son, Alfred. The bullying is lowering his self-confidence and hurting his grades in school. I could almost feel her pain.

Paul: Wow. People don't understand the amount of emotional pain that bullying can cause the entire family until they or someone they know is put into that situation.

Paulette: I don't recall ever having any bullying issues with our kids. Do you?

Paul: No. We did a great job in raising our kids…we were involved parents, provided good schools, lived in a caring community and maintained plenty of two-way communications.

Paulette: So…you mean we were fortunate and lucky.

Paul: Yep.

YOUR POINT OF VIEW?

_____
_____
_____
_____
_____
_____
_____
_____
_____
_____
_____
_____
_____
_____
_____
_____
_____
_____
_____
_____
_____
_____
_____
_____

CAPITALISM

Paulette: Paul. I am beginning to believe that American capitalism is not meeting our country's needs today. Instead of competition leading to a greater good for most people, today's capitalism mostly rewards those already at the top. That's why the top 400 wealthiest Americans have accumulated more wealth than 155 million other Americans combined.

Paul: Well...most Americans must spend every nickel they get their hands on to survive. You can't accumulate wealth that way. That's why we need to expand capitalism in a way which creates better paying jobs.

Paulette: Sounds good. We do need better paying jobs. Most middle class wages have been eliminated with the loss of America's global manufacturing leadership. However, a more balanced form of capitalism and less dependence on the American consumer is also needed.

The bottom line is that we must determine how to sell more to other nations and compete intellectually as a nation, not just as an elitist few.

Paul: I agree. But, unfortunately the political, financial and educational systems we have in place today do not support or encourage broader intellectual participation by the masses...it's not exactly what the founding fathers had in mind.

YOUR POINT OF VIEW?

CAREERS

Paul: Paulette?

Paulette: Yes, Dear?

Paul: It's not publically known, but tomorrow we are going to announce the layoff of another 5,000 professional associates from North American operations. No need to say, this has been a demanding week for me.

Paulette: How many layoffs in your Division, Paul?

Paul: Fortunately only 40, but half are senior people in their 50's and 10 are African-American men.

Paulette: Why so many older employees and aren't minority employees with engineering degrees difficult to hire?

Paul: Due to restructuring, mergers and cost cutting these days, age and seniority protects fewer employees. Diversity is not the same as Affirmative Action. The fact that whites are less likely to be laid off than nonwhites is not a serious company concern these days either. No real penalties. In addition, oversight these days, even by senior management, is not taken seriously like back in the 1970's and 1980's.

Paulette: Thank goodness we have not experienced job and career loss. It must be devastating to your sense of self-worth.

Paul: Thank goodness that corporate culture favors people like us and that we are liked.

YOUR POINT OF VIEW?

_____

_____

_____

_____

_____

_____

_____

_____

_____

_____

_____

_____

_____

_____

_____

_____

_____

_____

_____

_____

_____

_____

_____

_____

CELEBRITY

Paulette: Sweetheart. I unfortunately got into an argument with Josie this morning during our weekly phone chat. Sometimes I can't believe that she is my daughter.

Paul: What were you two arguing about this time?

Paulette: Well, I told her that I believed that celebrities have become a powerful influence on vulnerable people because of the position they have been given in our society and their economic status. Josie disagrees and believes that celebrities can be good role models for young people.

Paul: Maybe you both are right?

Paulette: Not on this one. I have concluded that she is wrong for two good reasons.

Paul: ...and they are?

Paulette: Well, first, the obsession with celebrity culture is not good for the country as a whole. Only a few kids will have a serious shot at becoming the American Idol or The Voice...and even fewer have a chance at becoming an All-pro athlete, a star recording artist or a movie star. Nevertheless, so many of our young people are so obsessed with becoming a celebrity of some sort that it distracts them from focusing on their education and a "real" career.

Paul: ...and the second reason?

Paulette: Most celebrities are Liberals.

YOUR POINT OF VIEW?

CHOICES

Paul: Paulette, are you awake?

Paulette: Yes, Dear.

Paul: I attended a conference today which centered on life choices and happiness. I have been under the impression that the more options we have in life the better. However, a recent study indicates that this might not be true. The study actually shows that abundant choice often makes for misery.

Paulette: I have never told you this Paul, but...I have always dreaded the times in my life when I had to choose between more than two options. I would always feel that I had a greater chance of making the wrong decision.

Paul: Well, I am glad that when you decided to marry me you had only two options...yes or no.

Paulette: Paul, there was actually a third choice that I have never mentioned. My ex-husband pleaded with me to consider re-marrying him.

Paul: You could have chosen not to share that with me...you know.

Paulette: Sorry...Sweetheart.

YOUR POINT OF VIEW?

CHILDREN

Paul: Oh, boy. I am really looking forward to getting some rest tonight.

Paulette: Had a long day, Paul?

Paul: Not really…but I did have a long discussion with our son, David. He and his wife, Jeanette, are trying to decide whether or not they should have children.

Paulette: Is he out of his mind? Of course they should have children. I have always dreamed of spending quality time with our grandchildren and spoiling them. Are they having marital or reproductive problems?

Paul: No. They are just considering how they want to spend the rest of their lives. They don't believe having children is necessary to have a happy marriage.

Paulette: It's not just about their lives and their marriage. We have a right to have grandchildren and they have the responsibility to please us.

Paul: Interesting. I didn't know that you felt that way. This is quite a dilemma.

YOUR POINT OF VIEW?

CHURCH

Paul: Are you prepared for your staff meeting tomorrow, Dear?

Paulette: Yes. It will consume most of my Monday morning.

Paul: You know...the attendance at Mass was really down today.

Paulette: Yes, it was. According to a Gallup Poll gauging trends among American Christians, weekly attendance among Protestants has been fairly steady over the past six decades. However, attendance among Roman Catholics dropped 30% over the same period.

Paul: Did they indicate the cause?

Paulette: Possible contributors were cultural upheaval of the 1960s, changes to the church brought about in the 1960s by the Second Vatican Council and national publicity since 2002 over sexual abuse lawsuits against Catholic priests.

However, only 43% of all Americans attend any type of religious service regularly.

Paul: So, despite the public and political rhetoric, active religious participation remains a minority interest in American life.

Paulette: Yep.

Paul: That explains the Sunday traffic jams at movie theaters, shopping malls and food stores.

YOUR POINT OF VIEW?

_____
_____
_____
_____
_____
_____
_____
_____
_____
_____
_____
_____
_____
_____
_____
_____
_____
_____
_____
_____
_____
_____
_____

CITIZENSHIP

Paul: Paulette. I must admit I am really disturbed by the fact that Newsweek gave 1,000 Americans the U.S. Citizenship Test and 38 percent failed.

Paulette: Why does that disturb you so much, Paul.

Paul: Because over 29 percent couldn't name the vice president. Seventy-three percent couldn't correctly say why we fought the Cold War and 44 percent were unable to define the Bill of Rights.

Paulette: But, civic ignorance is nothing new. For as long as we've existed, Americans have been misunderstanding checks and balances and misidentifying their senators.

Paul: I know. But, times have changed…and they've changed in ways that make civic ignorance a big problem in terms of both domestic challenges and America's global competiveness.

U.S. citizenship should mean more than simply being born here or passing a citizenship exam. I believe the main contributors to the nation's overall education dilemma are our decentralized education system and the failure of the country, as a whole, to realize the social and economic perils associated with broadly undereducated citizens.

Paulette: I agree. The problem is ignorance, not stupidity.

YOUR POINT OF VIEW?

_____
_____
_____
_____
_____
_____
_____
_____
_____
_____
_____
_____
_____
_____
_____
_____
_____
_____
_____
_____
_____
_____
_____
_____

COLLEGE

Paulette: Well, Sweetheart. How was your day?

Paul: Oh…great. However, I did read a disturbing article today in an educational journal that stated that the U.S. now ranks 12th among 36 developed nations in the number of 25 to 34 year-olds with college degrees. We once led the world in this category.

Paulette: The U.S. ranks 12th? You are kidding.

Paul: No…and the Bureau of Labor Statistics projects that seven of the 10 employment sectors that will see the largest job gains over the next decade won't require much more than some on-the-job training. These include home healthcare aides, customer service representatives, food preparers and servers.

Paulette: Then, why spend tens of thousands of dollars on higher education, often taking on huge debts along the way, when the job market doesn't seem to need you.

Paul: Because a college education is the ticket to the American Dream.

Paulette: Sounds like a nightmare.

YOUR POINT OF VIEW?

_____

_____

_____

_____

_____

_____

_____

_____

_____

_____

_____

_____

_____

_____

_____

_____

_____

_____

_____

_____

_____

_____

COMPETITION

Paulette: Paul. I am not sure why, but I have had this debate going on in my head all day regarding whether competition is good or bad?

Paul: Well…competition is the lifeblood of American society. It is celebrated as a virtue at all levels. It fuels business and determines who succeeds and who does not. School itself has become an arena for competition. Students compete with one another for a high position on the infamous "grading curve" which means that some will fail simply because others succeed.

Paulette: That is my concern. In order to have winners we must have losers. Also, the research I read this morning indicates that, from biology to psychology, experts agree that unbridled competition compromises individual health, threatens the quality of community life and increases inequality.

Paul: Intellectually, I agree. Without some level of restraint, competition can become destructive to institutions and individuals. So, competition is probably both good and bad.

Paulette: Oh, great. Good or bad versus good and bad…even more for my mind to debate.

YOUR POINT OF VIEW?

_____

_____

_____

_____

_____

_____

_____

_____

_____

_____

_____

_____

_____

_____

_____

_____

_____

_____

_____

_____

_____

_____

COMPUTERS

Paul: Well, Sweetheart. Did you get your shopping done today?

Paulette: Sure did. But, the computers were down at the grocery store this afternoon. It took 45 minutes for the clerk to check me out and he was using a calculator. And even then, I had to help him get the tax correct.

Paul: That's amazing. In little more than a half a century, computer technology has changed almost every aspect of our lives.

Paulette: I understand and value how computers have made it easier for us to access a wealth of information and have all but rendered printed encyclopedias obsolete. But, it looks as if we are educating our populous to expect computers to do their thinking in much the same way we have grown to expect machines to do our manual hard work.

Paul: Well, if that happens, we are doomed as a society.

Paulette: No. It will be us few independent thinkers who are left that are doomed. The rest of America will be as happy as a clam…and with an IQ to match.

YOUR POINT OF VIEW?

_____
_____
_____
_____
_____
_____
_____
_____
_____
_____
_____
_____
_____
_____
_____
_____
_____
_____
_____
_____
_____
_____
_____

CONSERVATIVE

Paulette: I was listening to Washington Journal on CSPAN before I left for work this morning and was surprised to hear so many partisan and bias phone calls.

Paul: Well…the Conservative Party has done a great job of painting the Democrats as big spenders and the champions of big government. As a fiscal Conservative, I am glad to see the Tea Party hold the old Republican guard to their pledge to slow down government spending.

Paulette: Liberals and Conservatives will always differ on the optimal size of government, but they should both come to an agreement that nothing in life is free.

Paul: Now, Paulette. Are you suggesting we increase taxes?

Paulette: No. But, I am saying that Liberals who want to spend and borrow for healthcare and social programs aren't any worse than Conservatives who want to spend and borrow for corporate subsidies and special interest.

Paul: True. However, being a Conservative is better off in one important regard.

Paulette: …and that is?

Paul: We and our family members have access to Medicare, Disaster Relief, Social Security and other social programs, if we ever need them, while enjoying the corporate and special interest perks as well.

Paulette: Well…sounds like the only win-win in American politics these days.

YOUR POINT OF VIEW?

_____
_____
_____
_____
_____
_____
_____
_____
_____
_____
_____
_____
_____
_____
_____
_____
_____
_____
_____
_____

CORPORATIONS

Paul: You know, Paulette…even as a Conservative, I am not sure I agree with the Supreme Court ruling which equates a corporation to an American citizen when it comes to the right to make campaign contributions.

Paulette: It is quite puzzling. If I recall correctly, when American colonists declared independence from England in 1776, they also freed themselves from control by English corporations that extracted their wealth and dominated trade. As a matter of fact, corporations were forbidden from attempting to influence elections, public policy and other realms of civic society.

Paul: So, how can we have such short memories?

Paulette: I would say…mostly due to American citizens not electing politicians who feel a need to protect the broader populous…along with unbridled corporate influence of elections, public policy and other realms of civic society.

YOUR POINT OF VIEW?

_____

_____

_____

_____

_____

_____

_____

_____

_____

_____

_____

_____

_____

_____

_____

_____

_____

_____

_____

_____

_____

DEATH

Paulette: Sweetheart. I am sure that Ginny would have enjoyed her homegoing service today. But…you know…it seems so hard to talk to anyone these days about death.

Paul: Well…Americans do not like to talk directly about death. In this country, people don't die, they "pass away," "expire" or "kick the bucket." Dead people are referred to as "loved ones." They are "laid to rest" rather than buried. People about to die are referred to as "terminally ill."

Paulette: Perhaps we have trouble talking about death because it is often so remote. People no longer die at home, but in nursing homes or hospitals. We are shielded from disease by medical science and before 9/11, we were insulated from the horrors of war by two great oceans.

Paul: Yeah. We have made death what sex once was…a subject only alluded to.

YOUR POINT OF VIEW?

_____

_____

_____

_____

_____

_____

_____

_____

_____

_____

_____

_____

_____

_____

_____

_____

_____

_____

_____

_____

_____

_____

DEMOCRACY

Paulette: Paul. What are we going to do for the fourth of July this year?

Paul: Well, along with the 4th being our wedding anniversary, it is also the birthday of American democracy. Maybe we can spend some time reflecting on the state of our democracy as we move into the second decade of the 21st Century.

Paulette: Interesting. What does democracy mean to you?

Paul: To me, democracy means freedom and the responsibilities that come with that freedom.

Paulette: ...and those are?

Paul: Well...the responsibility to be educated and informed, the responsibility to vote, the responsibility to give back to the community and the responsibility to listen openly to opposing points of view as well as learn from them.

Paulette: I agree. Democracy is a way of living and working together based on freedom, equality, justice and mutual respect. However...I also agree with Winston Churchill's assessment of democracy.

Paul: Which is?

Paulette: To paraphrase him, "democracy is the worst form of government...except for all the others."

YOUR POINT OF VIEW?

_____

_____

_____

_____

_____

_____

_____

_____

_____

_____

_____

_____

_____

_____

_____

_____

_____

_____

_____

_____

_____

_____

_____

DIETING

Paul: Hey, Sweetheart. I wrapped up my annual physical exam with my doctor this morning by reviewing the results of the blood work.

Paulette: How did you do?

Paul: My LDL cholesterol is a little high. My doctor suggests that I modify my diet to include more dry beans, fresh fruits, whole grains and vegetables.

Paulette: Well...you won't be alone. Nearly one-fourth of Americans are currently dieting. One-third of the U.S. adult population is overweight and another 25% is considered obese. This makes 60% of the population potential targets for diets.

Paul: To be honest, I am not a big fan of dieting. Most health issues are genetic. I say eat, enjoy and be happy.

Paulette: Sounds good. But, overweight and obese people are at higher risk of heart disease, Type 2 diabetes, stroke and high blood pressure. According to the Johns Hopkins Bloomberg School of Public Health, if the upward trend in weight continues, 86% of Americans will be overweight or obese by the year 2030...with a related healthcare cost of around $960 billion.

Paul: Okay. Eat better, enjoy it and happily become less of a burden on society.

YOUR POINT OF VIEW?

DRUG WARS

Paul: Paulette. I was reading today that the term "War on Drugs" was coined by President Nixon in 1971. We have been dealing with the so-called "drug wars" for over 40 years. Yet, drug production, smuggling and distribution have exploded into a sophisticated multinational business estimated at $300-$400 billion worldwide.

Paulette: Yes…and many people would believe that "dealing" is the operative word in that statement.

Paul: I don't quite understand. What do you mean?

Paulette: According to a recent World Health Organization survey, the United States, which has been driving much of the world's drug research and drug policy agenda, stands out with higher levels of use of cocaine and cannabis, despite punitive illegal drug policies.

It appears that it's a war where Americans are "dealing" heavily in both prevention and consumption.

Paul: Interesting way to look at it. How can we win this war?

Paulette: Not sure. Most likely the same way we would attempt to eliminate any human addiction. Remove both the need and the source.

Paul: You mean eliminate both the profit and the profiteers?

Paulette: You got it.

YOUR POINT OF VIEW?

EDUCATION

Paulette: Hey, Honey. The keynote speaker at today's Chamber of Commerce luncheon referred to a recent study indicating that the U.S. is losing ground in education compared to the rest of the world. I didn't realize that among adults age 25 to 34, the U.S. is 9th among industrialized nations in the share of its population that has at least a high school degree.

Paul: Not good. However, the U.S. has the largest GDP, the most powerful military, the largest number of billionaires and spends more dollars per student on education than any other country with the exception of Switzerland.

Paulette: Okay. But, according to a recent report by the Organization for Economic Co-operation and Development, the U.S. ranks 14th in reading, 24th in math and 17th in science.

Paul: It just means that even as the most powerful and richest nation in the world, we still can't force everyone to read well, learn math and like science.

Paulette: I don't understand how you can reach such an elitist conclusion Paul Sigmund Schuhmacher.

This country has a child education system that is compulsory and competitively funded in total, yet we still trail most industrialized nations in the world.

Have you ever considered that it might have more to do with our patchwork of funding and lack of national standards?

Paul: You might have a case there.

YOUR POINT OF VIEW?

_____

_____

_____

_____

_____

_____

_____

_____

_____

_____

_____

_____

_____

_____

_____

_____

_____

_____

_____

_____

_____

_____

_____

_____

ENTERTAINMENT

Paulette: Had a good day, Sweetheart?

Paul: Oh, it was great. At lunch today, we were discussing how large the entertainment industry is in the United States. From motion pictures, theater, television, gaming, books, magazines and music to amusement parks, exercise and sports, the market in the U. S. represented close to a trillion dollars in revenue in 2010.

Paulette: That's huge. That figure is almost the equivalent to the entire gross national product of Canada or Australia…and unlike spending for the necessities of life; it's all discretionary and emotionally driven.

Paul: Also, not surprisingly, about 93 percent of Americans have bought entertainment-related goods over the past year.

Paulette: Obviously, it's good for the economy. But, my concern is for those who seem to get so deeply immersed in entertainment that they begin to neglect the possibilities and responsibilities of the rest of their lives.

Paul: I understand. However, we all need rest, recovery time and enjoyable activities. Without some sort of stress relief, we would self-destruct.

Paulette: Yeah. You are right. I am sure that if we look at what most people have been doing most of the time throughout human history, it's probably not discussing moral philosophy and inventing calculus.

YOUR POINT OF VIEW?

_____

_____

_____

_____

_____

_____

_____

_____

_____

_____

_____

_____

_____

_____

_____

_____

_____

_____

_____

_____

_____

_____

_____

ENTITLEMENTS

Paulette: Paul. Are you awake?

Paul: Well…now I am. What's on your mind?

Paulette: I have been thinking about entitlement programs after listening to the President's speech on the topic earlier tonight.

Paul: As we have always agreed, some entitlements form genuine safety nets while others are hand-outs that should be scaled back or eliminated.

Paulette: I know what we have always thought. But after listening to the President talk about the "two strains" that have run through the country's political history and inform our political culture even today, I am torn as to which programs are truly not needed.

Paul: What did he say exactly?

Paulette: In summary, he reminded us that our strength as a nation has always been rooted in both our "individualism" and our "collectivism". In other words, we are a self-reliant people with a healthy skepticism of too much government. Yet, as a nation, we have always felt that through government, we should do together what we cannot do as well for ourselves.

Paul: Okay. Now, I see the dilemma. Distinguishing between hand-outs and genuine safety nets requires an unpretentious perspective of what we call entitlements, ourselves and the national good as a whole.

Paulette: Affirmative, my Dear.

YOUR POINT OF VIEW?

ENTREPRENEURSHIP

Paulette: Sweetheart. I have a presentation tomorrow to a group of bankers. I plan to firmly encourage them to loan more money to small businesses. It should significantly help reduce the unemployment rate. I have learned that being forceful on issues you believe in is the American way of doing things.

Paul: Well, all we hear from politicians and the news media these days is how the small business sector is going to propel the country out of this historical unemployment crisis.

Paulette: I know. But, I read a report today based on U.S. Census Bureau data which revealed that in 2009, only two percent (2%) of Americans working in private sector businesses were employed in companies started that year. Even young companies, those aged one-to-ten, only employed another 19.5 percent of private sector workers.

Paul: Are you going to share this information with the group of bankers tomorrow?

Paulette: Of course not. It's not my responsibility to correct the politicians and the news media for something that's not in my personal interest.

Paul: I agree. That's also the American way of doing things.

YOUR POINT OF VIEW?

_____
_____
_____
_____
_____
_____
_____
_____
_____
_____
_____
_____
_____
_____
_____
_____
_____
_____
_____
_____
_____
_____
_____
_____

EXERCISE

Paul: You know, Paulette. I really feel great since I started my morning exercise regimen. In addition to feeling stronger and having more stamina, I seem to be thinking quicker and clearer at work.

Paulette: Well…I read in a health magazine last week that not only is exercise smart for your heart and weight, but it can also make you smarter and better at what you do.

Paul: Interesting. I wonder how that works.

Paulette: I am not sure exactly, but from what I read, exercise leads to the release of certain neurotransmitters in the brain that alleviate pain, both physical and mental.

Paul: So, in addition to protecting us from heart disease and stroke, high blood pressure, noninsulin-dependent diabetes, obesity, back pain and osteoporosis, exercise can also improve our mood. Those are good reasons to maintain an exercise program throughout your life.

Paulette: I agree. But, despite the proven health benefits, seven out of ten American adults don't exercise regularly.

Paul: I wonder why it's such a hard sell to get everyone to maintain an exercise program throughout their life.

Paulette: Good question…it may be an inability to think quicker and clearer.

YOUR POINT OF VIEW?

_____
_____
_____
_____
_____
_____
_____
_____
_____
_____
_____
_____
_____
_____
_____
_____
_____
_____
_____
_____
_____
_____
_____
_____
_____
_____

FAILURE

Paul: Paulette. Need to share something with you.

Paulette: Yes, Dear?

Paul: You know the big European project that my Division has spent the last three years and a million dollars chasing and bidding.

Paulette: Yes...the NexGen computer. Oh. Did you guys win? That's wonderful!

Paul: No...our company president was secretly notified today that the European Consortium won. They seemed to have an insider's advantage throughout the bidding process. But, that's just how the contracting system works.

Paulette: Oh...you didn't win. I am so sorry. I know that you were counting on that project to keep your organization together.

Paul: Yep. I have a meeting with the Human Relations Department tomorrow to start developing the reorganization and reduction-in-force plans. I feel like such a failure.

Paulette: Don't feel that way. You gave it a good fight. You were as competitive as you could have been. Maybe the other company will fall flat on its face and you guys will get a second chance.

Paul: But, that's failure wishing for failure.

Paulette: Yes it is...only because I love you. Sorry...but, that's just how my system works.

YOUR POINT OF VIEW?

FAITH

Paulette: Oh, Sweetheart. What are your thoughts regarding the Father's message on faith in the 21st century this morning?

Paul: I thought he highlighted some interesting points. The point that really stuck with me is the appearance that a large number of Americans are placing less emphasis on believing and more emphasis on belonging.

Paulette: Yes, that was an interesting point. Especially since faith is the belief in God or in the doctrines of a religion, based on spiritual conviction rather than proof…and belonging is about closeness, familiarity & relationships with people.

Paul: I guess when you look at contemporary forms of worship today which include the use of modern Christian music; incorporating technology to project song lyrics, images, and video as part of the service; and the use of drama as a worship element, you can see how a feeling of belonging and association can become the leading attraction.

Paulette: Understand. However, from my personal perspective, worshipping acknowledges my identity and relationship with God and expresses my gratitude for what God has done. The more music, technology, drama and people involved…the better.

However…I worship because I believe.

Paul: Amen.

YOUR POINT OF VIEW?

FAMILY

Paulette: Paul. I have never asked you this before. However, after my conversation with Josie last night, I now need to know.

Paul: Need to know what, Sweetheart?

Paulette: How would you react if Josie and Janet decided that they would like to spend the rest of their lives together and have a family? I have been doing some research and learned that an estimated 65,500 adopted children are living with a Lesbian. That number includes 16,000 in California.

Paul: Well. Quite frankly, I haven't thought much about Josie and Janet having a family. I don't really know how to put this, but…do Lesbians have the biological desire to get pregnant and become a mother?

Paulette: Yes. Lesbians do have the biological desire to get pregnant and become mothers. If anything, they are probably more inclined to want children because, like Josie and Janet, most have the same biological instincts that heterosexual women have. For anyone to assume that lesbians do not desire children and a family is actually prejudging them just because they are Lesbian. They are still women and seek much of the same companionship, same commitment and same life as straight women.

Paul: I honestly don't get it. But, if Josie wants that kind of family, it's fine with me. Love makes a family, not biology or gender.

YOUR POINT OF VIEW?

_____

_____

_____

_____

_____

_____

_____

_____

_____

_____

_____

_____

_____

_____

_____

_____

_____

_____

_____

_____

_____

_____

FAMILY VALUES

Paulette: What are thinking about, my Dear?

Paul: You know...it's interesting that as we approach the 2012 Presidential election, the Conservative media is full of stories regarding the National debt, the deficit, the Tea Party and taxes. We have heard little about the staple of the Republicans' political strategies for three decades.

Paulette: What staple are you referring to?

Paul: Family values.

Paulette: Yeah. You are right. It's been a while since I have even heard the term. How did the term family values become a part of the political landscape anyway?

Paul: The use of family values as a political term became widespread after a 1992 speech by Vice President Quayle that attributed the Los Angeles riots to a breakdown of family values. Quayle blamed the violence in L.A. as stemming from a decay of moral values and family structure in American society. Thus, because of its political and contentious origin, it has been frequently used, mostly by Conservatives, in political debate.

Paulette: Only in politics can something that most Americans agree on and believe is the basis for a successful society become twisted and used in a contentious fashion.

Is a positive change in political discourse in this country even possible?

Paul: Politics without contention...what a novel idea.

YOUR POINT OF VIEW?

FATHERHOOD

Paul: Paulette, are you there?

Paulette: Of course I am.

Paul: As a part of my new charity board member role, I was asked to meet with a young man today who heads an organization he founded called "Fathers Guiding Fathers". He claims to travel around the country conducting workshops to help men accept the financial and physical responsibility for their children. Of course, he is asking us for a charitable donation.

Paulette: What reason did he give you to question him?

Paul: Well…First of all he is African American and secondly, I am not sure if this is where we should invest charitable dollars. Most likely, its primarily just black families affected.

Paulette: You are so wrong on both counts, my Dear.

Yes. Recent surveys suggest that only 20 to 25% of white students report fatherless homes in comparison with 56 to 60% of black students.

But, in total, children and youth from fatherless homes account for 63% of all youth suicides, 85% of all children that exhibit behavioral disorders and 71% of all high school dropouts. In addition, fatherless families are America's single largest source of poverty.

Paul: Okay. I stand corrected on both counts. What you described is not only bad news for all Americans, but should be viewed as a national epidemic. I will get back with Mr. Simms tomorrow to get the application started.

YOUR POINT OF VIEW?

_____
_____
_____
_____
_____
_____
_____
_____
_____
_____
_____
_____
_____
_____
_____
_____
_____
_____
_____
_____
_____
_____
_____

FINANCIAL SECURITY

Paulette: Sweetheart. Have you finished your pop?

Paul: Almost.

Paulette: By the way, David called me at the office today.

Paul: What did our son want?

Paulette: He wanted to schedule a meeting with me to discuss the plan he and Jeanette have put together to ensure that they are financially secure as they reach retirement.

Paul: I am glad to see our kids beginning to plan for their future. But, I am not sure if anyone in this country, other than the ultra-rich, can actually say that they are financially secure. With the potential of lengthy job loss, increasing cost of healthcare, sinking home prices, falling interest rates on savings and risky investments combined with increasing longevity...the average American today can't feel too secure.

Paulette: True. You can't control what you can't control. But, it is possible to feel secure.

Paul: ...and what are you going to tell David and Jeanette?

Paulette: That the goal of their plan should be to become debt-free, to always be in control of their expenses; to consistently increase their savings, assets and net worth on a monthly basis; and to prevent being forced to work at a job they dislike just to pay the bills.

Paul: I will drink to that.

YOUR POINT OF VIEW?

FOOD

Paulette: Paul. One of my co-workers has the cutest little four year old boy whose name is Eric. This morning Eric asked his mom, "Where does our food come from?" His mom said "The grocery store." Eric then replied, "No. I mean which country." Can you imagine a four year old asking such a question?

Paul: Sure. They are teaching the kids early these days about personal health and food safety. Food is one of the "life-lines" which protect our national security. Knowing how and when each food type enters our food supply is a major security factor.

Paulette: When our kids were growing up, I was glad that we lived is a state which grows so much of its own food. Do you remember the old Taylor Grocery Store down on 2nd Street? David and Josie really enjoyed going there to get the fresh corn.

Paul: Yep. Agribusiness is still one of Minnesota's largest industries.

Paulette: With the corn, soybeans, oats, wheat, barley, sugar beets and potatoes all grown here in the state, we could almost be self-sufficient.

Paul: ...and with the hogs, bison, elk and ostriches raised in the state, all we would need to import is oil.

Paulette: Well...there goes our self-sufficiency. Imagine...living in an America which has no need to fight to protect its oil "life-line" in the Middle East.

Paul: Self-sufficiency was a nice thought.

YOUR POINT OF VIEW?

_____

_____

_____

_____

_____

_____

_____

_____

_____

_____

_____

_____

_____

_____

_____

_____

_____

_____

_____

_____

_____

_____

FREE ENTERPRISE

Paulette: Honey…when you hear the economic phrase "free enterprise"…what does it mean to you?

Paul: Competition.

Paulette: …and what do you mean by competition?

Paul: Competing for customers or markets within an economy.

Paulette: …and how would you define an economy?

Paul: …a city, a state, a country, a region, a continent…where are you going with this line of questioning?

Paulette: In a meeting today, we were discussing the role of government in free enterprise. Some of us believe that free enterprise is the freedom of individuals and businesses to operate and compete with a minimum of government regulation. Yet, others believe that today's global competition and the emergence of China as an economic power, requires the U.S. Government to play a more active role.

I noticed that in your description of free enterprise, you didn't mention the role of government.

Paul: Well…in the game of free enterprise systems, there are four active components: households, businesses, markets and governments. The government component is always a wild card. It's a card that is seldom played unless you find yourself on the losing end of "free".

YOUR POINT OF VIEW?

FRIENDSHIP

Paulette: I had to go to the ladies room and have a good cry today at work.

Paul: Why? What happened, Sweetheart?

Paulette: I remembered that today is the fourth anniversary of Ginny's death.

Paul: Yeah. You and Ginny were such great friends.

I remember when you hired Ginny to work for you at the bank. I remember the visits we made to Ginny and John's house during the holidays when they lived down the street from us. I remember the times you would go with Ginny to her son Marc's hockey games when he was small.

I also remember…when Ginny won tickets to the Tina Turner concert. I remember when Ginny and John were divorced. I remember when Ginny sold the house and moved to New Mexico to write her poems and find a new way of life. I remember when we visited Ginny in Arizona and Ginny made us her infamous meatballs for the last time. I remember you reading one of Ginny's poems at her funeral.

Paulette: Oh, Paul. I am going to cry again.

Paul: It's okay Sweetheart. Ginny deserves a second cry.

Paulette: No. This one's not for Ginny. It's for me. I was just thinking, as you were talking, about how much I would miss you if you were not in my life to share and enjoy all of my friendships.

YOUR POINT OF VIEW?

_____

_____

_____

_____

_____

_____

_____

_____

_____

_____

_____

_____

_____

_____

_____

_____

_____

_____

_____

_____

_____

_____

_____

FUNERALS

Paul: Paulette. Have you ever given any thought to your funeral?

Paulette: Wait a minute. You are calling me Paulette and asking me about my funeral...in my bedroom...at 11:30 at night. Should I be paying more attention here?

Paul: Oh, no. I was online earlier tonight and ran across some intriguing history on funerals in America.

Paulette: Quite frankly, I have never thought much about the history of funerals. I dread the idea of having to go to a funeral...especially mine.

Paul: No, seriously. Did you realize that before the Civil War, "home" funerals were the norm? It wasn't until the 1900's that funeral directors were recognized as a trade. Then, casket sales emerged, embalming was encouraged and funeral directors embraced their status in society as keepers of the public health.

Haven't we seen a lot of change over a short period of time?

Paulette: Yeah. But, thank goodness there is one thing that hasn't changed over time regarding funerals---for the dead nor for the living.

Paul: What's that?

Paulette: A good funeral still gets the "dead" where they need to go, spiritually and the "living" where they need to be psychologically.

YOUR POINT OF VIEW?

GENDER

Paulette: Paul. Are you happy that you are a man?

Paul: Of course I am. Why are you asking?

Paulette: My friend, Gloria Hawkins, shared with me a surprising question that she was asked by her seven year old granddaughter. Her granddaughter asked, "Would I be happier if I was a boy?"

Paul: ...and what was your friend's response?

Paulette: She said she told her "No, baby...God made you a girl so that you could be happy".

Paul: Smart answer.

However...I did read in a provocative paper last week that surveys indicate that American women are wealthier, healthier and better educated than they were 30 years ago, but indexes show the average woman is less happy than her mate.

Paulette: I don't buy that. That article was probably written by a man --- the nerve of some men. I am an average woman and I am extremely happy with everything about myself. You have observed me for the past 30 years...other than being married to you, why do you think I am so happy?

Paul: ...because God made you a girl.

Paulette: Smart answer.

YOUR POINT OF VIEW?

_____

_____

_____

_____

_____

_____

_____

_____

_____

_____

_____

_____

_____

_____

_____

_____

_____

_____

_____

_____

_____

_____

GOVERNMENT

Paulette: I am so sick of hearing about the government. Most news programs, special reports or newspaper articles these days have something negative to say about the government. Either it's too much government or too little government. It's the government's surplus or the government's deficit. Has this always been the case in American history?

Paul: Well…yes…ever since the words "We the people of the United States, in order to form a more perfect Union, establish justice, insure domestic tranquility, provide for the common defense, and promote the general welfare" were baked into the Preamble of the U.S. Constitution. It seems that we have always disliked and disapproved of the government we the people have elected.

Paulette: You know…when you really think about it, you are right. I wonder why that's the case.

Paul: Not sure. But to me, only "common defense" will ever be achievable. Today, we have a "representative democracy" that has been gerrymandered by a two-party, electoral system. It appears that no one, except the President, can be held accountable for addressing national issues in a nonpartisan manner … in order to maintain a more perfect Union. Today, it seems that it's all about politics---driven by re-election, money, special interest and ideology.

Paulette: You know…you're right…and unfortunately, it also seems that achieving a sense of "justice, tranquility and general welfare" is only possible, as a nation, after a 9/11 type tragedy.

117

PILLOW TALK CONSCIOUSNESS

YOUR POINT OF VIEW?

GROUP THINK

Paul: Sweetheart. Are you awake?

Paulette: I am now. What's on your mind? You have been tossing and turning most of the night.

Paul: I am upset with myself.

Paulette: Why?

Paul: Well…I believe I broke one of my own rules today. I got caught-up in company groupthink. I refused to hire a female engineer that would have fit perfectly in a role on a critical project at work.

Paulette: …and what was the reason for not hiring her?

Paul: During her interview, I noticed that she had a tattoo on her upper body. She had a low cut top and it was hard not to notice. Our Human Relations Department must have also noticed the tattoo. They didn't tell me that I shouldn't hire her, but I could feel the pressure from them on me to make the "right decision".

Paulette: Let's see…the loss of individual creativity, uniqueness, and independent thinking to minimize conflict. Yes. It sounds like you went along with the group and forfeited your independent thought.

It's definitely not what you normally do.

Paul: I know…I am usually better at not allowing my sight to fall below the neckline when I interview female candidates.

YOUR POINT OF VIEW?

GUNS

Paulette: You know, I have been thinking about the home invasion and robbery last week in our neighborhood. Maybe we should consider getting a gun.

Paul: Now, Paulette. We have never owned a gun.

Paulette: I know. But, I would feel safer if I knew that we were able to protect ourselves and not become hostages in our own home. In America today…that translates into having a gun.

Paul: I understand. But, I have mixed feelings regarding guns in the home. A recent study indicated that a gun in a U.S. home is 22 times more likely to be used in an accidental shooting, a murder or a suicide than in self-defense. It seems a better way to make Americans feel safer is not to arm them with guns, but to tackle the causes of crime…such as urban poverty, joblessness, drug addiction and racial & social divisions.

Paulette: Makes sense. However, guns are big business and big politics. Protecting the sale of guns and selling more guns is as American as apple pie. Without a gun, we are just sitting ducks.

Sorry…but, if they have guns, feeling safe means we must also have a gun.

Paul: I am well aware of the pervasive "gun-for-a-gun" logic in this country. God help us as a nation if that's the best we can do.

YOUR POINT OF VIEW?

HEALTH

Paulette: Sweetheart. I can't believe that I spent over three hours on the phone with Josie last night.

Paul: That has to be a record for you and your daughter.

Paulette: Believe me, that was not the plan. It was just that she needed someone to talk to regarding what she calls the biggest problem that she and the other nurses in her hospital have these days.

Paul: ...and what is that?

Paulette: Obese patients.

Josie said that on her floor more than half of her patients weigh over 300 pounds...and half of those are children under fifteen years of age. It appears that the problem is not only the associated health issues, like Type 2 diabetes, but includes the physical strength and psychological endurance required by the nurses to professionally care for them.

Paul: Wow...and it does not seem that there is any relief in sight. I hear that obesity is the leading health problem in the U.S. and reaching epidemic proportions.

What is Josie doing to address her situation and to protect her career? She needs that job.

Paulette: Pilates, yoga, weight lifting and prayer three times a day.

YOUR POINT OF VIEW?

_____

_____

_____

_____

_____

_____

_____

_____

_____

_____

_____

_____

_____

_____

_____

_____

_____

_____

_____

_____

_____

_____

_____

_____

HEALTHCARE

Paul: Hey, Sweetheart. We finally received all the bills from your knee replacement surgery. I am being told that without our health insurance, it could have cost us over $35,000.

Paulette: As we know, here in the U.S. we spend an estimated $2 trillion annually on healthcare expenses, more than any other industrialized country. Yet, we rank with Turkey and Mexico as the only industrialized countries without universal health coverage.

But, truthfully, and probably like most average Americans, I don't understand what's at the heart of America's healthcare politics.

Paul: It's actually quite simple, yet perplexing.

Conservatives say we have a private health care system. In fact, we have a mixed private/public system which includes Medicare, Medicaid and tax breaks for employer-based insurance plans.

Liberals think that Americans overwhelmingly despise the current health care system. But, while about three-quarters of Americans will agree, when asked, that the health care system is a mess, costs too much and needs major reform...more than eight in 10 say they are satisfied with their current medical arrangements.

Paulette: Okay. Now, I get it.

Political half-truths and the tension between collective unhappiness & individual satisfaction are at the heart of America's healthcare politics.

Paul: Sweetheart...you just broke the code.

YOUR POINT OF VIEW?

HOME FORECLOSURE

Paulette: At lunch today, Mary and I were discussing how many people we know that have lost their homes to foreclosure this year.

It's a shame that corporations can walk away from failing investments due to bad economic times without a blemish. Yet, hardworking Americans must bear the wrath of being punished by almost everyone for seven years.

Paul: Emotionally, I agree. Most homes during the recession were lost to foreclosure due to job loss and sinking market values. However, from a U.S. economic perspective, personal debt is not the same as corporate debt.

Paulette: What do you mean?

Paul: Corporate debt is represented by a CEO, who is paid millions to protect the company image and its ability to rebound and eventually repay its stakeholders. Bankruptcy and foreclosure are business strategies upheld by the courts.

While personal debt is only represented by a social security number whose image is portrayed by a credit score. A somewhat arbitrary score created by "for-profit" corporations and ballyhooed by financial and consumer-based corporations who see value in prioritizing their prey.

Paulette: Sad…but well said.

YOUR POINT OF VIEW?

HOMOSEXUALITY

Paul: Sweetheart…I have to share this with you. One of my managers hired a new engineer today and dropped by my office so that I could meet him.

Paulette: Is he a nice guy?

Paul: He seems nice enough. But, he is not all "guy".

Paulette: So, you think he is Gay?

Paul: I would bet my life on it. He was sweeter than sweet.

Paulette: Paul, I didn't know that you had an attitude regarding Gay people. You have never had an issue with your daughter, Josie, being a Lesbian.

Paul: It's not Gay people, its overt homosexual men. I can, in a foresighted way, see why a woman might be attracted to another woman. There is something about femininity that says closeness and bonding. I also can understand the need for close male companionship. But, how can a man snuggle up with another hard head?

Paulette: There are some recent studies that suggest a basic biological link between sexual orientation and a range of mental functions. But, the bottom line is all Gay people are human beings and should be treated as such.

Paul: Oh, I agree. I am just curious. I would never treat a homosexual rudely…unless he steps out of line. I am a veteran you know.

YOUR POINT OF VIEW?

_____

_____

_____

_____

_____

_____

_____

_____

_____

_____

_____

_____

_____

_____

_____

_____

_____

_____

_____

_____

_____

ILLEGAL DRUGS

Paul: Paulette. I read a report the other day which stated that, in 2005 the world GDP was $36 trillion (U.S.) and the illegal drug trade was estimated as only around 1% of total global commerce. Yet, it is believed that the illegal drug trade was responsible for 90% of the killings along the U.S. and Mexican border along with 85% of the shoplifting, 70-80% of the burglaries and 54% of robberies in the United Kingdom.

Paulette: That is incredible…and it's probably worst today.

Paul: Yep. One answer would be to cut back on the demand for illegal drugs. It seems that a significantly reduced demand would cripple the violent trade that sprouts up to supply it.

Paulette: It also seems that if we treated the use of illegal drugs as a public-health problem as well as a crime…it would move us in that direction.

Paul: Maybe. But, currently most of the U.S. anti-drug budget goes toward interdiction efforts and punishing people.

Paulette: Then, do you think we will eventually move toward the legalization of drugs as a means to curb the violence?

Paul: Sure…just as we did with alcohol. The question is: how many billions of additional dollars we will spend and how many decades we will waste, as a society, before we finally see legalization as the only way out of this society-generated mess?

YOUR POINT OF VIEW?

IMMIGRATION

Paulette: Sweetheart. It became obvious to me today during a lunch meeting that most Americans don't really know much about the U.S. Immigration Policy. They seem to think that it's all about the illegal influx of Mexican and Central American immigrants.

Paul: That's an excellent observation. Most Americans get what they know from the news media and politicians --- neither of which has an interest in educating the public beyond what's in their own best interest. The broader U.S. Immigration Policy contends that America has reaped tremendous benefits from opening its doors to short-time immigrants for high tech and low tech jobs.

Paulette: Then, why the recent uproar over Immigration Reform?

Paul: Because an estimated 13.9 million people now live in the U.S. illegally. Illegal immigration is being blamed as the cause of many economic issues we face today such as decreasing job opportunities for citizens, rising costs, injustice and crime.

Paulette: If that is true, why can't we, as a nation, just determine the best approach and simply fix the immigration problem?

Paul: For the same reason we can't fix the federal deficit, military spending, entitlement programs, social security, rising healthcare costs and reliance on foreign oil.

Paulette: Oh yeah, the 12 P's...Polls, Politics, Polarization, Prejudice, Preference, Persuasion, Propaganda, Pretense, Public apathy, Powerful Politicians and the unprecedented selfishness of the American People.

YOUR POINT OF VIEW?

_____
_____
_____
_____
_____
_____
_____
_____
_____
_____
_____
_____
_____
_____
_____
_____
_____
_____
_____
_____
_____
_____
_____
_____
_____

INTERNATIONAL AFFAIRS

Paul: Paulette. I was listening to talk radio this afternoon on my way home from work and the pundits were asking the question, "Do most Americans care about and understand America's foreign policy?"

Paulette: Well…I would think that after 9/11 the number of Americans who care has significantly increased. However, really understanding U.S. foreign policy and the importance of us managing international affairs versus allowing them to manage us is most likely far above the intellect of the average American.

Paul: Not to sound arrogant, and I wouldn't share this outside this room, but I must agree with you. The honest truth is that when it comes to our dependence on foreign oil, keeping jobs in the U.S. and protecting the country from terrorism like 9/11, I believe that most Americans get it. But, keeping informed of and influencing the foreign policy strategy that either creates or fails to prevent the crises we seem to find ourselves in, much too often, is above most of our pay grades.

Paulette: In other words, it is a little like suffering through the teenage years with your kids. You care a lot about the things that are going on in their lives that you understand. But, you can only pray a lot about those things that you do not understand but seem so important to them and their survival.

Paul: Bingo.

YOUR POINT OF VIEW?

INTERNET

Paulette: Sweetheart. I had to "half" apologize this afternoon to Nikki, my new social media community manager, after scolding her for not informing me that the Regional Bank meeting had been moved from 3:00 to 2:00. I walked in late and felt like an idiot.

Paul: Was it Nikki's responsibility to inform you of the change.

Paulette: Yes.

Paul: Then, why did you have to apologize?

Paulette: Because I learned later that she did send me an email message regarding the time change. But, when I was a young woman working for a vice president, I knew the importance of "making sure" that he or she was aware of all meeting changes. I knew that it was my responsibility to communicate in an "efficient and timely" manner. The young people these days just automatically assume that if they send you an email, a Tweet or a Facebook message that they have communicated with you.

Paul: So, what was the reason for only a "half" apology?

Paulette: Nikki is doing a great job in the new social media role for the bank. So, I wanted to send the right message.

Paul: Which was?

Paulette: She got it half right. The email she sent was efficient for her, but not timely for me.

YOUR POINT OF VIEW?

_____

_____

_____

_____

_____

_____

_____

_____

_____

_____

_____

_____

_____

_____

_____

_____

_____

_____

_____

_____

INSURANCE

Paul: You know...Paulette. I was glad to hear that the fundraiser for Iggy Castro was able to raise half of the cost for the kidney transplant he so desperately needs. He was so embarrassed to ask for help.

Paulette: Who is Iggy Castro?

Paul: Oh...Iggy is an old acquaintance who worked at my company for over twenty-years. Unfortunately, he was caught in one of the rounds of downsizings a few years ago.

Paulette: I assume he does not have health insurance.

Paul: No. At 56 years old, he was not able to find another job and could not afford to maintain health insurance...and wouldn't you know it...he then started to have kidney problems.

Paulette: That's too bad. I read in a report that there has been significant erosion in employer-sponsored insurance over the last decade...from 69% to 61%. Hardest hit are low and moderate income families.

Paul: Yep...those who can't afford to buy health insurance coverage in the current market.

Paulette: I have never told you this. But, even though I am a Republican, I pray that healthcare reform is not repealed but just strengthen. I can't imagine what it's like to become a second class citizen, simply because you lose your job and get sick.

Paul: I have never told you this...but, ditto.

YOUR POINT OF VIEW?

INTELLIGENCE

Paulette: Sweetheart. I am tired. It's time to cut the lights out. What are you reading?

Paul: A very interesting report. It indicates that the U.S. scores the lowest in national average Intelligence Quotient (IQ) among the developed countries of the world. According to this report, we have a national average IQ score of 98. A score of 98 is below 22 countries…including Switzerland, United Kingdom, Germany, Japan, North Korea and China.

Paulette: You're kidding. What's their definition of intelligence?

Paul: Let me read it: "Intelligence is a person's capacity to acquire knowledge (i.e., learn and understand), apply knowledge (solve problems) and engage in abstract reasoning."

Paulette: So, it sounds like it is the power of a country's intellect and a very important aspect of a country's overall well-being.

Paul: I would say so…and for the wealthiest nation in the world to rank near the bottom among other industrialized countries is a little puzzling.

Paulette: It must be the method used to get a national count. You know that the U.S. is known for having difficulties with national counts, especially when the country's well-being and "hanging chads" are involved.

YOUR POINT OF VIEW?

JOBS

Paulette: Paul. I got a call today from my friend Clara. She was crying.

Paul: What was wrong?

Paulette: Her husband Art was let go from his job yesterday as a part of a corporate downsizing, after 23 years with the same company. You know she lost her job only a few weeks ago.

Paul: Wow, that's hard. It's funny that job loss is just something you hear about in the news until that job belongs to you or someone close to you.

Paulette: Yeah. 9.1 percent unemployment doesn't seem like a big deal when you are among the 90.9 percent of the working population. Do you realize that 9.1 percent unemployment translates into about 14 million people? Also, around 30 million family members are affected. That many Americans without an adequate means to support themselves sound almost wicked.

Paul: Well...as James Meade, the economist once said, "In the 1930s one was aware of two great evils...mass unemployment and the threat of war".

YOUR POINT OF VIEW?

_____

_____

_____

_____

_____

_____

_____

_____

_____

_____

_____

_____

_____

_____

_____

_____

_____

_____

_____

_____

_____

_____

_____

LABOR UNIONS

Paulette: Paul. Isn't it interesting how Politicians and many other Americans are supporting overt actions which seem aimed at dismantling labor unions? In recent news coverage, it appears that teachers and municipal workers are being blamed for causing the Great Recession by making $32,000 a year and agreeing to trade higher compensation for health insurance and retirement benefits.

Paul: The union movement has never been well received in America. Since the American Revolution, Americans have held true to the concept of "rugged individualism."

Paulette: What is rugged individualism?

Paul: Back then, it was the common feeling that it was acceptable for individuals, known as Industrialists, to own the means of production and to exploit the labor of men, women and children as long as the opportunity existed for anyone in America to rise to that level.

Paulette: Is that where the phrase "rags to riches" originated?

Paul: Yes. Wealth through hard work and ingenuity was okay, in spite of labor exploitation and inhumane conditions.

Paulette: Well…if America's future is without some type of collective bargaining for the working class and if corporations and governments are allowed to continue to act more and more like "Industrialists", it sure seems like the average American will see more rags and less riches.

YOUR POINT OF VIEW?

LEGACY

Paulette: Honey. I thought the meeting today with our attorney was a good one. I feel better about our decision to do some legacy planning.

Paul: So do I. At first, I was not sure about the idea. But, the more I learned about what's involved in legacy planning, the more comfortable I am that this is the right thing to do and now is the right time to do it.

Paulette: Let's see…you agreed to work on the letter to the Executor of our estate, a letter to our family members and a master list of our records. I agreed to start work on the family stories, recipes, scrapbooks and photo albums.

Paul: That's correct. You know, I originally thought that legacy planning was just a new name for estate planning. But, having a way to preserve our values, memories and final wishes as well as to ease the burden of our eventual passing on to our children is a good thing.

Paulette: Yes. What David and Josie will value most is not what we owned, but the evidence of who we were and the tales of how we loved.

Paul: Thanks for pushing us into this Sweetheart.

Paulette: Thanks for loving all of us, my Dear.

YOUR POINT OF VIEW?

_____

_____

_____

_____

_____

_____

_____

_____

_____

_____

_____

_____

_____

_____

_____

_____

_____

_____

_____

_____

_____

_____

_____

_____

LIBERAL

Paulette: Today, I watched a news special on the poor in America. Did you realize that one of our monthly pay checks is equal to what Health & Human Services has established as the annual poverty threshold for a family of six in this country?

Paul: No. I didn't know that.

Paulette: Well...according to this report, last year, roughly 4 million people joined the ranks of the poor in America and the gap between the rich and the poor continues to widen. What do you think is the reason for the growing disparity?

Paul: Being a Conservative, I tend to believe that becoming impoverished is primarily driven by a lack of motivation to help oneself which is made worse by government aid and entitlements.

Paulette: ...and if you were a Liberal?

Paul: Well, Liberals attribute the growing levels of poverty to factors such as a poor economy, lack of affordable housing and lack of good schools and resources necessary for teaching and developing the basic skills required, at a minimum, to apply for employment.

But...as a Christian, I would have to agree with the Liberals on this one.

Paulette: This has to be a first...why?

Paul: Because God created man in his own image...and my God is not a lazy God. If a lack of motivation to help oneself is the cause of poverty in America, then its origin is here on earth.

YOUR POINT OF VIEW?

LIFE

Paulette: Paul, are you okay?

Paul: Yes. I am fine. Thanks for asking, Sweetheart.

Paulette: Your Mom would have been proud of you and your brothers today. It was a wonderful funeral service.

Paul: I miss her so much already. She was an amazing woman.

Paulette: We all miss her. However, at 87, she had a wonderful and long life fueled by the happiness that she received from you guys.

Paul: It's interesting that you would say that. I had a long conversation with Mom just prior to our wedding. I asked her what she believed to be the fuel for a meaningful life. Without hesitation, she said "happiness".

Paulette: Oh, really?

Paul: Yes…and she added that happiness has two frames, the present moment and the future. She said "if we live in the now and not think about the future, life would be bliss. On the other hand, if we only think about the future, we're never going to enjoy what's right under our nose." Then, she said, "That's why it's so important for us to have faith in God. It's our faith that allows us to achieve both present-moment happiness and joy about the future."

Paulette: She was an amazing woman.

YOUR POINT OF VIEW?

_____

_____

_____

_____

_____

_____

_____

_____

_____

_____

_____

_____

_____

_____

_____

_____

_____

_____

_____

_____

_____

_____

_____

_____

LOVE

Paulette: Sweetheart. I know that this might sound a little like girly stuff, but I must share this with you.

Paul: Now, let me decide that. What is it?

Paulette: The topic at the Women's Club meeting today was how to recognize the difference between "loving someone" and "being in love" with someone. I am ashamed to admit that we carried on for hours without a clear differentiation that we all could agree on.

Paul: Well, from a man's perspective that's easy. "Loving someone" is normally out of reciprocity. Such as me loving you because you love me or loving your family members and friends because they love you.

Paulette: ...and "being in love"?

Paul: "Being in love" means that everything that was once mine is now ours; thinking of you and us versus me; wondering what would make us happy instead of what would make me happy; and doing things that I would not normally do because it's what you want to do.

Paulette: Now, I really know why I chose to marry you.

YOUR POINT OF VIEW?

MARRIAGE

Paul: Sweetheart?

Paulette: Yes, Paul.

You know…in a few weeks we will be celebrating our 34th wedding anniversary. At times, I am at a loss for words when it comes to describing our marriage and its importance to me.

Paulette: Oh, Paul. You are so sweet. Not to put you on the spot, but how would you describe our marriage?

Paul: Well…I see our marriage as a life-long commitment to love and take care of each other. I see our marriage as the foundation upon which we, as individuals, have been able to stand and truly reveal ourselves to each other.

I also see our marriage as the institution from which we have been allowed to grow as individuals and together as a couple over the past 33 years.

Most importantly, I see our marriage as having elevated us from friends to partners to a blessed union. Because of the relationship our marriage has allowed us to establish, I don't know where I end and you begin.

Paulette: Enough said. Would you please turn out the lights and come over here.

YOUR POINT OF VIEW?

MEDIA

Paul: I was listening to NPR this morning and heard a group of media commentators stirring up the divisiveness in the country.

They were insisting that what the American people want in the upcoming presidential election are "red meat" candidates vs. those that are conciliatory. Even as a Conservative, I was shocked to hear a respected media outlet allow this type of barbarianism.

Paulette: Honestly, I am not surprised. The U.S. media landscape is dominated by massive corporations. In many cases, these giant companies are vertically integrated and control everything, from production to final distribution. Even NPR must find it hard to resist the pervasiveness of the divisive tone these corporations skillfully broadcast for their own selfish purposes.

Paul: How did we as Americans allow this to happen?

Paulette: By allowing mergers and acquisitions, we have given concentrated control over what we see, hear and read to a few very wealthy people and their handful of well-paid news editors.

Paul: But, the U.S. Supreme Court, in the landmark 1969 case of Red Lion v. FCC, said "...the First Amendment preserves...the right of the public to receive suitable access to social, political, esthetic, moral, and other ideas and experiences..."

Paulette: Yes. But access is not control... and, in reality, the Internet is no match for the influential mainstream TV, radio and news media when it comes to reaching the "voting" public.

YOUR POINT OF VIEW?

MEN

Paul: According to a magazine article I read today, among the male population, there are more 20-year-olds in America right now than any other single-age group…and the second largest single-age group is 50-year-olds.

Paulette: That's a surprise. So, there are mostly 20 and 50 year old men available for most middle-aged women. It doesn't seem that those two age groups have much in common.

Paul: Well…according to a survey there were a few things that 20-year-olds and 50-year-olds seem to agree on.

Paulette: …and they were?

Paul: The joy of watching football, the coolness of Clint Eastwood, gun control and the death penalty.

Paulette: …and the things they seem to disagree on the most?

Paul: Off-shore drilling and how much they're willing to pay for a suit.

Paulette: …Not what I would call stimulating interest in either case. But, at least the poor women in the 30 and 40 year old age group have something to use as they either "look up" or "look down" to find a man. Not much…but something.

PILLOW TALK CONSCIOUSNESS

YOUR POINT OF VIEW?

_____
_____
_____
_____
_____
_____
_____
_____
_____
_____
_____
_____
_____
_____
_____
_____
_____
_____
_____
_____
_____
_____
_____
_____

MILITARY

Paulette: Sweetheart. I must confess that as a banker, I know nothing about the military and its relationships. I heard a discussion on cable news about the Military Industrial Complex.

What is it anyway?

Paul: Well...the Military Industrial Complex is a concept referring to policy and monetary relationships between legislators, national armed forces and the industrial sector that supports them.

Paulette: The news commentator also referred to this Complex as a type of "iron" triangle. Why?

Paul: Well...the Military Industrial Complex is viewed by many, who really understand the relationships, as a threat to the interest of the country as a whole. The Complex has also been referred to as a precursor to Fascism --- a radical, authoritarian nationalist political ideology.

Paulette: A set of relationships that is a threat to the interest of the country and could lead to Fascism...you must be kidding.

Paul: No. These relationships include political contributions, political approval for defense spending, lobbying to support bureaucracies and beneficial legislation and oversight of the industry.

Paulette: Oh, my God. Those kinds of relationships between three politically powerful groups with vested psychological, moral, and material interest...they are right...a "formidable" triangle.

YOUR POINT OF VIEW?

_____

_____

_____

_____

_____

_____

_____

_____

_____

_____

_____

_____

_____

_____

_____

_____

_____

_____

_____

_____

MORTGAGES

Paulette: Hey, Honey. We met with an expert at the bank today to discuss what is most likely to be the future of home mortgages.

Paul: I assume that the recent recession and job losses are causing homeownership to evaporate for many Americans.

Paulette: Yep…and the prospect of major changes in home finance could mean a bigger chunk of Americans will be locked out of the housing market. That's also bad news for current homeowners. They will have a harder time unloading their property.

Paul: With recent discussions of possibly eliminating the mortgage interest tax write-off in the future, it might be worth considering the trade-off associated with renting versus buying a home.

Paulette: Our bank's analysts show that if you stay in your home for six years, buying is better. However, some analysts are predicting that 15 to 20 percent down payments could become the norm.

Paul: Well, if that happens, I wouldn't be surprised to see as many as a third of potential homebuyers shut out and will have to rent regardless of the trade-off.

Paulette: You are correct. We have already reduced our mortgage department at the bank by a third. In the future, more "homes sweet homes" will be rentals.

Paul: Yep. I wonder how this will affect the daily lives and net worth of the average American.

YOUR POINT OF VIEW?

_____
_____
_____
_____
_____
_____
_____
_____
_____
_____
_____
_____
_____
_____
_____
_____
_____
_____
_____
_____
_____
_____
_____
_____

MOTHERHOOD

Paulette: Paul. I know that you and your mother were close. Did you two ever talk about what kind of person she expected you to be when you grew up?

Paul: It's funny you ask. I do recall when I was about twelve I asked mom if she wanted me to be a musician or an engineer. Instead of just telling me what she thought, she said, "Give me a couple of days to think more about it".

Paulette: Well, did she ever tell you?

Paul: Not really. But, a week or so later she asked Patrick, Peter and me to join her for a walk into town. During that walk, she shared with us what she thought any mother would want from her children.

I remember the conversation as if it was yesterday. She said something like…"I want you kids to be self-sufficient and to learn how to be resourceful. I want you to know how to ask questions, seek answers, speak up for yourselves when you have to and hold your tongue when it's best not to speak. I also want you to learn how to express and channel your emotions."

She also said, "But most of all, I want you to stand up, be strong, look within and apply the grace and common sense that God gave you."

Paulette: That's almost exactly what I told David and Josie when they were around twelve years old.

Paul: …must be the universal message of motherhood.

YOUR POINT OF VIEW?

_____
_____
_____
_____
_____
_____
_____
_____
_____
_____
_____
_____
_____
_____
_____
_____
_____
_____
_____
_____
_____
_____
_____

MOTIVATION

Paulette: Hi Sweetheart. How did your golf game with David go today?

Paul: Golf was okay. However, we spent an hour after the game discussing a challenge that David is currently having at work.

Paulette: What kind of challenge?

Paul: He has not been able to motivate his engineering design team to work on weekends to ensure that they meet a critical project deadline.

Paulette: Just let them know that if they don't get it done, he'll fire them.

Paul: It's not that easy. Since management increased employee healthcare benefit contributions and eliminated the company contribution to their 401Ks, it seems that many employees have become divisive and dogmatic. David is just the team lead. His actions to alleviate the acute dissatisfaction are limited.

Paulette: Then, what are his options?

Paul: Well, he basically has to demonstrate his enthusiasm, inspiration, dedication, drive, desire, impetus and commitment to completing the project on time and hope it serves as an incentive to others.

Paulette: That sounds like the only options that were available to the President last summer during the Federal deficit show down with a divisive and dogmatic Congress.

Paul: You know…I agree.

YOUR POINT OF VIEW?

MUSIC

Paulette: Sweetheart. I made our reservations for the first week in October for this year's Oktoberfest.

Paul: Oh, great. I believe that this will be the 29th consecutive Oktoberfest held in New Ulm.

Paulette: ...and just think...your mother played piano for the Concord Singers who were the foremost, amateur, German language singing male chorus in America back in the 1950's.

Paul: It is nice to be able to still listen to and enjoy the festive German music that I grew up with in a live setting. To hear oldies these days, you have to turn to recorded music.

Paulette: True. However, the Financial Times recently reported that consumers, world-wide, spend less money on recorded music today than they did in the 1990s, including digital downloads. This dramatic decline in revenue has caused large-scale layoffs inside the industry, driven retailers out of business and forced record companies and record producers to seek new business models.

Paul: Wow. I didn't realize the significant decline in the music industry. I assume that recording artists have also been hit hard.

Paulette: Yes. Recording artists now rely on live performance and merchandise for the majority of their income.

Paul: ...as did the Concord Singers back in the 1950's.

YOUR POINT OF VIEW?

OBESITY

Paul: Sweetheart. I can't stop thinking about a man I saw at the restaurant where we took some Chinese customers to lunch this afternoon.

Paulette: What was it about the man that made such a lasting impression, my Dear?

Paul: He must have weighed 500 pounds. One of his legs was as big as one of my customers. They had to put two tables together for him. He ordered enough food to feed four people…and would you believe that he had the nerve to order dessert.

Paulette: Paul, those are not nice things to say.

Paul: I know. I would never tell anyone else this. But, my God…why can't people just pull themselves away from the dinner table?

Paulette: Paul…I know that seems logical, but…it's not that easy. Obesity is far more complex. Obesity is not always caused by simple behavioral issues. For instance, genetic determinations such as the way a body expends energy, hormones that affect the way calories are processed and other body organ activity can all affect appetite.

Paul: I understand. But, according to The Centers for Disease Control and Prevention the main causes of obesity in America are imbalanced diets and calories from eating too much.

Paulette: I can't disagree with that, Sweetheart. But, try to be a little more tolerant of those who are battling that demon. I am sure that it's not easy for them to look at "skin and bones" and "lean muscular physiques" all day either.

YOUR POINT OF VIEW?

_____

_____

_____

_____

_____

_____

_____

_____

_____

_____

_____

_____

_____

_____

_____

_____

_____

_____

_____

_____

_____

_____

_____

PARENTING

Paulette: Paul. I had lunch today with three ladies who have young families. I could not believe some of the parenting techniques they admitted using on their kids. I am afraid parenting is in trouble.

Paul: I don't quite understand. What do you mean?

Paulette: Well…when we were raising our kids we did listen to some advice of experts. But, we knew how we were raised and how we turned out. So, we raised our kids to be us.

Nowadays, it appears a generation of young parents actually missed being "parented". So, they don't have a clue and only have the insight of so-called experts. For example, they are being told that spankings will make their children more aggressive, that criticism will destroy their self-esteem and that children who feel loved will be kinder and more loving to others.

As a result of this advice, most parents today are administering far fewer spankings and reprimands and far more physical affection and praise, than their grandparents did.

Paul: Well, are today's children less aggressive, kinder, more self-confident or happier than the children of two generations ago?

Paulette: Far from it. Rates of childhood depression and suicide have gone up, not down, and there has been no decline in aggressiveness. According to a recent study, every 1 second a high school student is suspended, every 9 seconds a child drops out of school and every 4 minutes a child is arrested for drugs.

Paul: Okay. I see what you mean. Parenting is in trouble.

YOUR POINT OF VIEW?

_____

_____

_____

_____

_____

_____

_____

_____

_____

_____

_____

_____

_____

_____

_____

_____

_____

_____

_____

_____

_____

_____

PHILANTHROPY

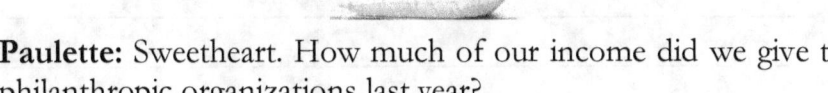

Paulette: Sweetheart. How much of our income did we give to philanthropic organizations last year?

Paul: Not sure. But, including the church, I would say at least 10 to 15 percent. Why do you ask?

Paulette: Doing my board meeting today at the Girls Home, we were discussing the results of a recent survey which indicates that more Americans have stopped donating to charities. There seems to be less motivation to help others in need than in years past.

Paul: Interesting. Frankly, I believe that most Americans are only motivated by selfish reasons…such as tax deductions, community recognition and being seen as a good corporate citizen.

Paulette: You might be right. It would nice to believe that people were motivated by a deeply held need to find a meaning in life which comes from an intertwined community connection.

Paul: That's a wonderful description of true philanthropists. But, in difficult economic times, the average American is deeply intertwined with job loss, rising gas prices and avoiding home foreclosure. It's an unfortunate situation for everyone.

Paulette: I know. We are closing the Girls Home at the end of the year. After months of campaigning and fundraising we can't replace the reduction in Federal funding. But, it's still nice to believe that in better times there will be more true philanthropists.

YOUR POINT OF VIEW?

POLITICS

Paulette: Hey, Sweetheart. I was listening to a debate on talk radio today regarding term limits for all politicians and I began to wonder how we would fill all the positions in the country if term limits became a reality.

It seems like more "ordinary people" who care about and will represent the country as a whole...like you and me...would have to serve a term in public office.

Paul: Well...expanded use of term limits might be possible at the local and state level. But, at the U.S. congressional level, there are two main reasons why term limits will never happen.

Paulette: ...and they are?

Paul: First of all, our two-party system has "gerrymandered" or fixed the congressional districts throughout the country such that they are either majority Republican or Democrat. That's why despite Congress, as a whole, having an approval rate of 17%...around 90% of congressmen are re-elected each cycle. Everyone likes their own Congress person and Congress people like to be re-elected.

Paulette: ...and the second?

Paul: With so much money and power now involved in politics, it has become somewhat a "career of royalty" for many politicians.

Paulette: So, no room for "ordinary people" who care about and will represent the country as a whole.

Paul: Nope.

YOUR POINT OF VIEW?

_____
_____
_____
_____
_____
_____
_____
_____
_____
_____
_____
_____
_____
_____
_____
_____
_____
_____
_____
_____
_____

POVERTY

Paulette: Honey, give me your hand. I want to say a prayer.

"Lord, thank you so much for protecting me, my husband and our family. Thank you for ensuring that we did not lose our jobs during the last recession and do not have to experience what so many Americans are experiencing for the first time in their lives. Please ease their discomfort and give them the strength to hold on until this storm passes. In the name of your son Jesus Christ, we say Amen".

Paul: I know that you love the Lord, but what was that all about?

Paulette: Well, I read a New York Times article earlier tonight about the recent recession and the so-called "new poor" in America. I just can't stop thinking about the "sobering message".

Paul: What did the article say?

Paulette: This recovery will leave more people behind than in past recessions due to record-setting ranks of the long-term unemployed. People accustomed to the comforts of middle-class life are now relying on public assistance for the first time and potentially for years to come. They are being called the "new poor".

Paul: …and the sobering message?

Paulette: If it wasn't for the grace of God, we could have been among them.

Paul: Here…take my other hand.

YOUR POINT OF VIEW?

PRAYER

Paulette: Sweetheart, listen to this --- "According to a USA TODAY/Gallup Poll of 1,000 adults, 92% say there is a God and 83% say this God answers prayers."

Paul: That's good to hear. 100% would be even better.

Paulette: Yep. The same poll indicates that a majority of Americans want to believe in a higher power and want to believe that someone or something out there can do things that they cannot do for themselves. It is interesting that most Americans say that they pray for health.

When you pray, what do you pray for?

Paul: Well, first of all, I believe that God is accessible, listens and is the source of my emotional and psychological well-being. So, I always start by giving the Lord thanks for waking me each day with a reasonable amount of physical strength and mental health.

Then, I pray for you, other members of our family, our friends, our neighbors and the sick & shut-in. I pray for employment, patience, wisdom, peace and goodwill on earth as well as for the spiritual strength for me to stay focused and to trust my faith.

Paulette: That's a wonderful prayer, my Dear. Amen.

YOUR POINT OF VIEW?

_____

_____

_____

_____

_____

_____

_____

_____

_____

_____

_____

_____

_____

_____

_____

_____

_____

_____

_____

_____

_____

_____

_____

PREJUDICE

Paulette: Sweetheart. We hired a new project manager today at the office. But, my instincts tell me that he might not fit in well with my team and the corporate culture.

Paul: Who was the idiot who hired this misfit anyway?

Paulette: He was hired by Greg Cooper, our VP of Global Services. Greg was the company's first Black employee.

Paul: Oh. So now you have a pair of them.

Paulette: Paul, please. That sounds like a racist comment. If I used language like that in the office, it would probably sound discriminatory and it could cost our company a lot of money.

Paul: Not as much as a company's racist corporate culture could cost people of color because they are instinctively viewed as not able to fit in.

Paulette: You know, I have never thought of it that way.

Paul: Well…our Human Relations Department trains us to not act simply on instinct when it comes to hiring decisions. It's only human nature to instinctively be more comfortable with what is familiar than what seems foreign.

Paulette: Excellent point. It's amazing how something that obvious is…so easily overlooked or ignored.

Paul: …and so costly.

YOUR POINT OF VIEW?

_____

_____

_____

_____

_____

_____

_____

_____

_____

_____

_____

_____

_____

_____

_____

_____

_____

_____

_____

_____

_____

_____

PRESCRIPTION DRUGS

Paulette: It was so nice to speak with Aunt Mattie this afternoon.

Paul: Oh, you spoke with Mattie.

Paulette: Yes. She was released from her treatment at the Betty Ford Center last week and seems to be doing quite well.

Paul: That's good to hear. When will they know if the drug addiction treatment was successful?

Paulette: For God's sake, let's hope it works. The 90-day treatment program cost Aunt Mattie over $50,000.

Paul: You know…prior to Mattie's episode, I wasn't aware that prescription drugs are the second most commonly abused category of drugs, behind marijuana and ahead of cocaine, heroin, methamphetamine and other drugs.

Paulette: Yep…and the growing population of aging Baby Boomers are prime candidates for prescription drug abuse, intentional or not. Once we begin taking pills for things like managing blood pressure and cholesterol, it becomes easier to take narcotic pain killers, prescription sleep aids and other more addictive drugs.

Paul: Sweetheart, let's agree to watch each other for possible risk of prescription drug addiction as we get older.

Paulette: That's a great idea…now…before it gets too late, what about that thing I have been addicted to for 34 years.

YOUR POINT OF VIEW?

PRISON

Paul: Paulette. I spoke with my brother Peter today. He will complete his 18 month sentence at the Federal Prison Camp at Pensacola in a couple of months.

Paulette: Poor, Peter. I still can't believe he got caught up in that Ponzi scam. Now, he is a convicted felon.

Paul: Never in my dreams would I have imagined Peter a felon. Darn it …and he will still be on probation for a year.

Paulette: Well…according to a U.S. Bureau of Justice Statistics report, at year-end 2009, there were over 7.5 million people on probation, in jail or on parole. That's about 3.1% of adults in the U.S. resident population. So, Peter won't be alone.

Paul: Sweetheart. I should share this with you. I have been meeting with Father Travis over the past two years in an attempt to find a way to stop feeling guilty for not being a better brother to Peter.

Paulette: Paul Schuhmacher. You had nothing to do with the choices Peter made. Please stop beating yourself up for something that was never in your control.

Paul: I know, Paulette. But, he's my baby brother and I love him so much…and I feel so bad for him.

Paulette: Stop the tears and get some sleep. We can talk more about this later.

YOUR POINT OF VIEW?

_____
_____
_____
_____
_____
_____
_____
_____
_____
_____
_____
_____
_____
_____
_____
_____
_____
_____
_____
_____
_____
_____

PRIVILEGE

Paulette: Paul, are you still awake?

Paul: I am now. What's up?

Paulette: Today, I read a study which indicates that when it comes to knowledge regarding the U.S. government, foreign students often put American students to shame…and would you believe it's being shrugged off by the majority in America as irrelevant. They just don't see or admit to the challenges we have in education in this country, as a whole.

Paul: That level of ignorance and arrogance is not surprising to me. It's a predictable consequence of majority privilege in this country. Privilege is typically invisible to those who have it.

Paulette: You mean that Whites and men tend not to see privileges because they are taken to be normal entitlements.

Paul: Yes. That is how things appear to members of a dominant group.

Paulette: Is this why us women often know more about you men than you know about yourselves and why minorities know more about whites than whites know about themselves?

Paul: Yes. But, privilege is not without costs. Unfortunately, the mirror with which to view ourselves is lost.

Paulette: That's insightful…yet not encouraging.

YOUR POINT OF VIEW?

REAL ESTATE

Paul: We are fortunate that the Minnesota housing market wasn't as hard hit as California, Nevada, Florida, Arizona and other states.

Paulette: Yes. Thank goodness. Do you remember Marvin and Yvette Ackerman? I worked with Yvette at the old bank. They moved to Arizona several years ago when Marvin's job was transferred to the Phoenix area.

Paul: Not sure I do.

Paulette: Anyway, I spoke with someone close to Yvette today and learned that Marvin and Yvette were both laid off from their jobs a couple of years ago. Unfortunately, the home they bought there in 2005 for $300,000 is worth only $99,000 today. With the loss of income and the inability to sell the property, they will most likely lose their home to foreclosure…and they are our age.

Paul: I am not surprised. I just read an article that the U.S. hit a record in 2010 with over 1.2 million home foreclosures. The Bank Executives told Congress last year that they could see a $900 billion imbalance between mortgage liabilities and the decline in market values due to the housing crash and resulting recession.

Paulette: So, the Banks and Congress decided to just allow homeowners to bear all of the burden, shame and pain for the worst residential real estate mess in history.

Paul: You got it. Even as a Conservative, I must admit the whole thing smells.

PILLOW TALK CONSCIOUSNESS

YOUR POINT OF VIEW?

_____

_____

_____

_____

_____

_____

_____

_____

_____

_____

_____

_____

_____

_____

_____

_____

_____

_____

_____

_____

_____

_____

REALITY SHOWS

Paulette: How was your day off? Did you relax and watch some TV like you wanted.

Paul: Well, I had to turn off the television. I can only take Housewives, Basketball wives and the Situation in small doses. It's true that people of our generation also grew up with what's now called Reality TV. However, a steady diet of today's gossip, undermining, arguing and fighting doesn't say much for most American's reality.

Paulette: What do you mean we grew up on Reality TV? I don't remember anything resembling Big Brother or the Kardashians.

Paul: Well, I would agree that the nosiness of Candid Camera was different than the "camera being on all the time" in the Big Brother house. The premise for both shows, however, is catching ordinary people in the act of doing interesting things. But, I laughed with the people on Candid Camera because it could have been me. I don't see any of "myself" in today's reality shows.

Paulette: Hmm. I never thought of those familiar old shows as Reality TV, but you're right. I wonder who do see "themselves" in today's reality shows…not very many people we know.

Paul: Good question. Certainly those who are willing to support the TV network's strategy to not pay actors and writers and to make record profits while depriving us of the quality prime time TV which once presented America at its best versus at its worst.

YOUR POINT OF VIEW?

RELATIONSHIPS

Paulette: Paul. Are you happy with us and our relationship?

Paul: Paulette, we've been married to each other too long for me to fall for that question. Of course, I am very happy with us. Now, why are you asking me that question?

Paulette: Well, we will be celebrating 34 years of marriage this year…and I read an article yesterday which stated that married adults now divorce two-and-a-half times as often as adults did 20 years ago and four times as often as they did 50 years ago. Most divorces were on the grounds of "irreconcilable differences".

I just want to make sure that our relationship does not have any of "those".

Paul: No. We don't have to worry about "irreconcilable differences" in our relationship.

Paulette: Why do you say that?

Paul: Because, we are quite compatible. Plus, one of us is quite skillful at avoiding potential areas of conflict, staying away from unnecessary clashes and mitigating opposing points of views.

Paulette: Thanks. Honey.

Paul: You are most welcome. Those are the only skills I learned during my officer's training in the military that were 100% transferable to civilian life.

YOUR POINT OF VIEW?

RELIGION

Paulette: Sweetheart. What did you think of the Father's message on James 2:4 about not discriminating or showing favoritism?

Paul: Well, there are many in this country who would like to see more church leaders and Christians take a leadership role on other national social and economic issues in the same fashion they voice their opposition to abortion and Gay marriage.

Paulette: Do you think that with the current political gridlock and the magnitude of today's economic & social issues, more church leaders and Christians will move in that direction?

Paul: Nope. It will never happen.

Paulette: Well…why are you so confident of that?

Paul: Church leaders depend on Church members for financial support in order to preach the Word. Along with professing to be Christians, their members are also Republicans, Democrats, Independents, Libertarians, Tea Partiers, Conservatives, Liberals, pro-universal healthcare, anti-universal healthcare and so on.

Paulette: Oh. So, you are saying that Sunday is the time to listen to the Word and agree on how we should live. But, Monday is the time to listen to the media, politicians & distorted public opinion polls and decide how we will live.

Paul: Unfortunately, that's the case…not consistent with James' view of…how to live as a Christian.

YOUR POINT OF VIEW?

_____

_____

_____

_____

_____

_____

_____

_____

_____

_____

_____

_____

_____

_____

_____

_____

_____

_____

_____

_____

_____

_____

_____

SCHOOL

Paul: Paulette. I read in the local paper this morning that they're talking about lengthening the school day for K-12.

Paulette: I am aware of the debate. I am steadfastly on the side of longer school days. Neuroscience has shown that it's the combination of genes and early life experiences that determine how the brain wires itself. Hopefully, longer school days will mean more diverse experiences and stronger minds for the kids.

Paul: Yes. I wonder if it could have the same positive mental effect for adult learners.

Paulette: The challenge is that when most Americans reach adulthood, they end up having the same experiences, with the same people, in the same places, putting out the same level of effort and getting the same results. Not much new is learned.

It seems that it's all about only being around people who express your own point of view.

Paul: Yeah. Those darn genes.

YOUR POINT OF VIEW?

_____

_____

_____

_____

_____

_____

_____

_____

_____

_____

_____

_____

_____

_____

_____

_____

_____

_____

_____

_____

_____

_____

SECURITY

Paul: Okay, Sweetheart. It's time to turn out the lights. What are you reading?

Paulette: An article which has a quote from Helen Keller.

Paul: Which quote is that?

Paulette: "Security is mostly a superstition. It does not exist in nature, nor do the children of men as a whole experience it. Avoiding danger is no safer in the long run than outright exposure. Life is either a daring adventure, or nothing."

Paul: ...never heard that one. What's the premise of the article?

Paulette: The title is "What Do You Need to Feel Secure?" The premise is that some people define security "internally" while others define security "externally".

Paul: What's an example of feeling secure externally?

Paulette: When you need time to get external factors in order before acting, such as more money in the bank or a house fully paid off.

Paul: ... and feeling secure internally?

Paulette: When you are entrepreneurial-minded, confident in your own abilities and acting spontaneously.

Paul: Well...I am feeling internally secure at the moment and need some daring adventure. Now...turn out the lights and come on over here.

YOUR POINT OF VIEW?

SELF AWARENESS

Paul: I noticed this morning that my hairline is starting to recede further.

Paulette: Oh. Sweetheart, it's probably no big deal. But you might want to check with a trichologist and make sure everything's in order.

Paul: I have also been noticing that I have to get up at least once at night now. As you know, I used to sleep through the entire night without having to go to the rest room.

Paulette: Oh. Sweetheart, it's probably no big deal. But you might want to check with your urologist and make sure everything's in order.

Paul: ...and believe it or not I have been experiencing a little shortness of breath during my morning walks.

Paulette: Oh. Sweetheart, it's probably no big deal. But you might want to check with your cardiologist and make sure everything's in order.

Paul: I wonder if this is what George Sheehan meant when he said "The mind's first step to self-awareness must be through the body."

Paulette: I seriously doubt it, Paul. But...I might want to check with our Trust attorney tomorrow to make sure everything's in order.

YOUR POINT OF VIEW?

_____

_____

_____

_____

_____

_____

_____

_____

_____

_____

_____

_____

_____

_____

_____

_____

_____

_____

_____

_____

_____

_____

_____

SEX

Paulette: Sweetheart. At lunch today, we were discussing a recent American Psychological Association study which reported that girls and young women suffer intellectual, psychological and physical problems as a result of television and other commercial messages that push sexualization.

Paul: Sexualization? What does that mean?

Paulette: Sexualization is defined as a "person's value coming only from his or her sexual appeal or behavior, to the exclusion of other characteristics."

Paul: That's interesting. How do you feel about that?

Paulette: I feel that when a person is held to a standard that equates physical attractiveness with being sexy, he or she is being sexually objectified.

Paul: Sexually objectified? What does that mean?

Paulette: That is, made into a thing for others' sexual use, rather than seen as a person with the capacity for independent action and decision making.

Paul: Sexualization sounds brutal…it should be outlawed.

YOUR POINT OF VIEW?

SOCIAL MEDIA

Paulette: Paul. I found out today that the bank has given me the responsibility for launching a new social media team and has assigned to me a social media community manager.

Paul: You mean like Facebook, Twitter and that kind of thing? Why is the bank fooling around with that stuff? It's just for young folk who spend hours every day on a computer or a smart phone.

Paulette: Yes and no. My primary responsibility involves using social media tools and platforms to create a community with our customers. Social media is taking the world by storm, and if you haven't jumped on this bandwagon, you're going to be left behind.

Paul: I must admit that at sixty-three years of age, I am not exactly on the bandwagon. But, I understand how social media integrates the technology, social interaction and the use of words, video and audio. What I am struggling with, at my age, is "why"?

Paulette: Because it is available. The corporations behind it are spending a lot of money pushing the platforms and smart phones to use it. Like it or not, as millions of people around the world get connected online in this fashion, social media will be the way to reach them, shape their thoughts in your direction and eventually sell them your goods. My bank must be online, engaging with intelligent users and getting them to "like us" in order to win our market share.

Paul: It sounds like you are ready…and plan to take no prisoners.

YOUR POINT OF VIEW?

_____

_____

_____

_____

_____

_____

_____

_____

_____

_____

_____

_____

_____

_____

_____

_____

_____

_____

_____

_____

_____

_____

_____

SOCIALISM

Paul: You know, it seems that whatever the President talks about---whether it's overhauling health care, or regulating Wall Street, or telling schoolchildren to study hard---his opponents call him a socialist. Why do you think this is occurring and so loudly?

Paulette: Well. Based on what I have read over the last several months, there are two things that come to mind.

Paul: ...and they are?

Paulette: First of all, when any American reform leader takes on the status quo, he or she confronts a well-organized and reactionary opposition. It's no surprise that the right-wing of our Party now compares the President to Hitler and likens his healthcare reform to socialism?

Secondly, it's the President's race. The recent accusations of socialism from some conservatives echo similar accusations leveled at black leaders in the past, as though the quest for racial parity were simply a left-wing plot.

Paul: That's very astute of you...and does not reflect well on 21st Century American politics and some American attitudes and prejudices that just will not die.

Paulette: ...and, unfortunately, some of these enduring attitudes and prejudices are being given second lives with the deliberate use, on talk radio and in the national media, of code words like "take our country back" and "Obamacare".

YOUR POINT OF VIEW?

_____

_____

_____

_____

_____

_____

_____

_____

_____

_____

_____

_____

_____

_____

_____

_____

_____

_____

_____

_____

_____

_____

_____

SOCIAL SECURITY

Paul: Your sister Margaret called this morning. It was nice to speak with her. I didn't realize that she turned 65 last month. She said thanks for your help with the social security issue.

Paulette: Yes. I spoke with my friend at the Social Security Administration last week. He confirmed that Margaret will not be able to draw any social security benefits.

Paul: Why is that?

Paulette: She has not earned enough Social Security "credits."

Paul: Social Security credits…what are those?

Paulette: You earn credits by working and paying Social Security taxes. If you were born in 1929 or later, you need 40 credits or 10 years of work to qualify. Margaret taught school for 9 years and 8 months prior to starting her family. With John's successful career, she never had to return to work. Fortunately, his cancer treatment prior to his death, only wiped out half of their savings.

Paul: Any other way she can get Social Security benefits?

Paulette: Become disabled or blind and have resources (real estate, bank accounts, cash, stocks and bonds) that are worth no more than $2,000.

Paul: So, what else can Margaret do? She's only 4 months short of having earned enough Social Security credits.

Paulette: She starts her greeter's job at Walmart on Monday.

PILLOW TALK CONSCIOUSNESS

YOUR POINT OF VIEW?

_____
_____
_____
_____
_____
_____
_____
_____
_____
_____
_____
_____
_____
_____
_____
_____
_____
_____
_____
_____
_____
_____
_____

SOCIETY

Paul: By choosing to use technology to create TV ratings and "going viral" prospects for social media, our society is cheating our next generation of the opportunity for more global competitiveness.

Paulette: I'm sorry, Dear. But, what the heck are you talking about?

Paul: Oh. I was watching ESPN today and the discussion was about a college athlete, videotaped making unsubstantiated comments about his school's recruiting policies. As a result, within minutes, the video was being broadcasted all over the sports networks, cable news, Facebook and Twitter.

Paulette: So…

Paul: So, the football coach interviewed regarding the incident got it right. He said, "Listen…the kid made a mistake, he apologized and it should not have been such a big deal. However, in today's world of 24-hour news and social media, we are forced to provide our young athletics with a TV coach, a Facebook coach and a Twitter coach. What is our society coming too?"

Paulette: I see your point. For media content and ratings today, we use technology to create controversy about irrelevant aspects of our society when we could be using the opportunity to enhance the intellectual and true social capacity of the members of our society in order compete more effectively globally.

Paul: You are better at words than I am…but that's what I was trying to say.

YOUR POINT OF VIEW?

SPORTS

Paulette: Sweetheart, my sister Lillie is really concerned about her grandson, Michael. But, I am concerned she's getting too involved in trying to raise the kid since his father died.

Paul: What's wrong with young Michael?

Paulette: He will turn 10 years old next month and he has shown no interest in any sports activity.

Paul: Does Lillie think he is Gay?

Paulette: No, of course not. According to Lillie, Michael is more interested in computers and video games. She seems to think that her daughter, Laura, is raising a geek.

Paul: Wait a minute. I would suggest that Lillie back away and let Laura raise her son. If Lillie shares that attitude with Michael, he might grow up with a low opinion of himself and she will see him as a failure because he isn't the grandson she wanted.

Paulette: I see your point. Most kids Michael's age have similar interests. Computers and games are part of most kids' lives today.

Paul: I also believe that participating in sports activity is important for the physical fitness and mental growth of a child. But, Michael deserves a mother...and grandmother...who will love him and appreciate him for who he is.

Paulette: You are right...and who knows. Michael might grow up to be the next Mickey Mantle...and then again, the next Bill Gates.

YOUR POINT OF VIEW?

STOCK MARKET

Paulette: Sweetheart. Did we exercise all of the stock options today?

Paul: I met with Jerry, our stock broker. We set all of the sell price windows. We should know after the market opens tomorrow how well we have done. But, Jerry anticipates us ending up with at least a six figure gain on the total portfolio.

Paulette: Oh, that's great. How does it feel to be a millionaire?

Paul: The bottom line is that our companies' stock prices have increased significantly over the past 10 years; we have been fortunate to have received such a large number of stock options over that period and we had the patience to wait until now to sell.

Paulette: Now, the question is where will be put the cash after taxes to protect it from inflation and maybe even add to it until we need it for retirement.

Paul: I know. Interest rates on savings are still almost nothing, the real estate market is a bust and precious metals are not close to a sure thing.

Paulette: Well, we have another 10 to 12 years before we fully retire. In order to maintain our current lifestyle in retirement, we will still need to add to our retirement fund.

Paul: Okay. I will call Jerry tomorrow and ask him to identify some new stocks for a pre-retirement portfolio.

YOUR POINT OF VIEW?

_____
_____
_____
_____
_____
_____
_____
_____
_____
_____
_____
_____
_____
_____
_____
_____
_____
_____
_____
_____
_____
_____
_____
_____

STUPIDITY

Paul: I found myself in a very disturbing situation this afternoon when I stopped by Mr. Yee's cleaners to pick up my suits.

Paulette: What happened, Sweetheart?

Paul: Mr. Yee was in the backroom having a loud argument with his son. I couldn't really determine what the argument was about, but he kept shouting, "You are stupid, you are stupid".

Paulette: Oh, that's terrible.

Paul: Yea. To call anyone stupid, and certainly your son, seems extreme. I wonder if it is just a language nuance. Some people tend to use the word stupid without truly understanding the difference between stupidity and ignorance.

Paulette: I totally agree…and in our world of ever changing sound bites, acronyms and abbreviations, there is certainly the opportunity for any of us to appear ignorant at any given time.

Paul: I recall my mother telling us when we were young, that "Ignorance is not knowing and stupidity is knowing and doing it anyway."

Paulette: I have always viewed ignorance as being caused by the circumstances of one's life, whereas stupidity is due to an attitude problem or mental deficiency.

Paul: Anyway…I will have a talk with Mr. Yee the next time I stop by the cleaners.

YOUR POINT OF VIEW?

SUCCESS

Paulette: Hey, Honey…do you feel we have been successful?

Paul: I think so. What's on your mind?

Paulette: Oh…this morning when I was looking in the mirror, I noticed that my face has begun to reflect, what I call "experience".

Paul: Huh…that's a good way to put it. But, to me you are more beautiful now than the day I married you.

Paulette: You are so sweet. However, that's not my point. While looking in the mirror I asked myself. "Paulette, does your face reflect that you have achieved the goals you have set for yourself in life?"

Paul: Good question. In my opinion, achieving goals in life is important… but that's not how I would define success. To me, a goal is a destination…while success is a journey.

Paulette: …Would you help me with that trend of thought, please?

Paul: Sure…when you arrive at one of life's destinations, you stop, take a deep breath and say, I made it. However, you know that you are successful in life when you can look back at each stop…enjoy them in hindsight…learn from them…and then use those stops to plan and be excited about your next destination.

Paulette: So, if I am successful, the "experience" I see in the mirror each morning will reflect where "I am headed" versus "where I have been."

Paul: You bet…now head over here and let me enjoy some of that success.

YOUR POINT OF VIEW?

TAXES

Paul: Sweetheart, I picked up our tax return this afternoon from Bill, our CPA.

Paulette: Okay, Dear. How did we do last year?

Paul: Bill was able to get our effective tax rate down to 16% from a possible maximum rate of 35%, including that darn AMT tax.

Paulette: Wow. This makes about ten years in a row that we have decreased our Federal tax payments. How did he do it this time?

Paul: The reductions included our personal exemptions; deductions for state and local real estate taxes; deductions of sales and excise taxes on the new car; the mortgage interest on our home; the mortgage interest on the lake house; losses we decided to take on the stock we sold; losses we had from year-one investments in the Real Estate Trust; the energy tax credits for the installing the storm windows; the rather large charitable contribution to our church; the donation to the local charter school; the gift we gave to the German Arts Festival and, of course, the extension of the Bush tax cuts.

Paulette: Well…in April, CNN reported that "for tax year 2010, roughly 45% of households, or about 69 million, will end up owing nothing in federal income tax, according to estimates by the nonpartisan Tax Policy Center."

Paul: Just shows that the Conservative mantra of "no more taxes" is working…at least for about half of the country.

YOUR POINT OF VIEW?

TECHNOLOGY

Paulette: Sweetheart. I watched an outstanding program on cable TV last night. It provided a chronicle of how the evolution of technology has changed society worldwide. However, the producers didn't draw a conclusion as to whether it has had a positive or negative influence. As a technologist, do you believe that the use of technology has helped or hurt American society?

Paul: Well, as technology has developed throughout the years, it has greatly affected society and the way people around the world live in many aspects. Has it been a good or bad influence for American society? I would probably say…both.

Paulette: In what ways?

Paul: I would say the three major aspects of our society that have been greatly affected by technology are communications, travel and business.

In communications & travel, technology has made our world smaller. Good in terms of providing Americans access to anywhere at any time. Bad in the sense that, terrorists and those who want to hurt Americans also have the same access.

Through the use of technology, business is now eternally global. Good in terms of American industry's access to customers around the world. Bad in the sense that, the good jobs, that were once concentrated in the U.S. are now scattered around the world.

Paulette: So, you could say that technology's impact on American society has been a double-edged sword.

Paul: Very much so…both figuratively and literally.

YOUR POINT OF VIEW?

TRAVEL

Paulette: Honey…our flight leaves at 7:30 in the morning. So, we need to get to the airport no later than 5:30 AM.

Paul: I know. It's a shame that we must get to the airport so early. I tell you, traveling these days is a real pain in the neck.

Paulette: I remember when we could get to the airport a half hour prior to flight time and have plenty of time to get through security and make the flight. Now, we must stand in line to check our bags, pay for our bags to come with us and then carry our bags over to the TSA---all prior to even getting to the terminal access area.

Paul: Yep. When we get to the terminal access area, we then must wait in another line to eventually take off our shoes, remove our belts and remove the little quart bag of toiletries & our laptops from our carry-on to place on the screening belt.

Paulette: …and God forbid the hassle if we forget to remove some coins from our pocket or have a knee transplant like myself. After all of the poking and searching and putting yourself back together, we are almost too tired to walk the half mile to the gate.

Paul: Then, once we are at the gate, we wait to board the plane, wait on the plane until clearance is provided for the flight to take off and wait until the plane reaches 10,000 feet in altitude before we can use the rest room.

Paulette: Whew…I am tired just thinking about it. Good night, Sweetheart. I need to get some rest.

YOUR POINT OF VIEW?

VOTING

Paul: Sweetheart. My friend, Andrew, recently shared with me an extremely surprising story regarding the voter registration process in this state.

Paulette: Really. What was it about the voter registration process and why was it so surprising?

Paul: Well. When Andrew and Gena moved into their new house in March, Andrew updated the address on his driver's license.

Paulette: Okay…there must be more.

Paul: Yes. In May, he learned that because he moved, six miles down the street, he had to re-register to vote. Of course, he thought when he updated his driver's license his voter registration would also be updated. So, he went through the process again and received his new voter registration card in the mail in June.

Paulette: And…there must be more.

Paul: Yes. In July, he received a letter in his post office box indicating that the local Recorders' Office had just recently received a forwarding notice from the post office and he would have to go through the voter registration process again within 35 days or his name would be automatically transferred to the "inactive' list.

Paulette: So, the fact that voting in the U.S. is local and extremely susceptible to errors, inaccuracy & silliness is a surprise to you?

Paul: No…the fact that this could happen to a Republican.

PILLOW TALK CONSCIOUSNESS

YOUR POINT OF VIEW?

_____
_____
_____
_____
_____
_____
_____
_____
_____
_____
_____
_____
_____
_____
_____
_____
_____
_____
_____
_____
_____
_____
_____
_____
_____

WAR

Paulette: I heard today that the U.S. military is now involved in the longest war ever with the operations continuing in Afghanistan. However, with the all-volunteer military and recent political decisions to fund wars with debt versus public sacrifice, most of us have been spared the real pain and cost of war.

Paul: You know, we were told in the military that General Sherman ineptly precipitated Civil War deaths to be as bloody and brutal as possible to drive home the point that failure to negotiate a compromise bore savagely inhumane results.

Paulette: …and your point being?

Paul: Similarly today, U.S. military action aboard and domestic "political warfare" at home is precipitating the bloody and brutal death of America's middle class…maybe due to a failure to negotiate a compromise.

Paulette: Is that because it's mostly middle class kids that are dying on the battlefield and middle class jobs, healthcare and retirement being slaughtered economically and politically here at home?

Paul: Yes…and by the inept use of our military, misuse of our tax dollars and the abuse of public trust by brutal politicians, savage special interest and inhumane ideologues.

Paulette: Wow. That's a mouthful.

YOUR POINT OF VIEW?

WEATHER

Paul: Wow, today was a hot one.

Paulette: Yes, it was Sweetheart. We have been experiencing weather extremes in all parts of the world lately. However, the concept of climate change and global warming is still being hotly debated.

Paul: The issue is how climate is defined.

Paulette: What do you mean? Isn't climate the same as weather?

Paul: Technically, no. Climate is the average of many weather events over a span of years. That's why scientists can't really say that climate change is "caused" by a single weather event, regardless of how devastating it might be.

Paulette: Well…what if you combine the European heat wave of 2003 which killed 70,000 people, the Indian Ocean tsunami of 2004 which killed 220,000 people, Hurricane Katrina of 2005 which killed 1,300 people, Cyclone Nargis of 2008 which killed 140,000 people and the Tsunami of Japan of 2011 which was responsible for over 24,000 deaths. That was a lot of weather and devastation over almost a decade. I do not believe that we have seen weather of this severity and frequency in our lifetime.

Paul: I understand. But, still, technically it doesn't substantiate global warming as a crisis.

Paulette: So be it…but, I am aware of at least 455,300 people that would disagree, if they were still with us.

YOUR POINT OF VIEW?

WOMEN

Paul: Paulette. I saw the announcement in the local paper regarding the new Vice President of Marketing that your Bank recently hired. It's funny you haven't said much about your new counterpart.

Paulette: Well, we've had lunch a couple of times. Her energy is infectious. She is not bad looking and has a good mind. I vaguely remember when I was a young 30-something Vice President.

Paul: So...she is cute, young and smart. But, I bet she doesn't have your legs and charm.

Paulette: That's why I love you. You know, I started out trying to be supportive but I don't think she takes counsel well. I think she is also managing to irritate our boss, Jerry, as well as the rest of the 24th floor. I don't mind that she is always checking that darn Blackberry for messages and never makes eye contact when I am trying to have a conversation with her. I am still determined to get to know her. Her knowledge should benefit the Bank, if she's able to learn the ropes and fit in. However, I don't believe that anyone else on the 24th floor will take the time to help her.

Paul: So, do you plan on coaching her and showing her the ropes?

Paulette: Well, you said it...she's cute, young and smart.

Paul: In other words...competition.

Paulette: Exactly.

YOUR POINT OF VIEW?

_____

_____

_____

_____

_____

_____

_____

_____

_____

_____

_____

_____

_____

_____

_____

_____

_____

_____

_____

_____

_____

_____

_____

WORK ETHIC

Paul: Sweetheart. How was your day?

Paulette: Oh, fine. I spent the afternoon as a part of a panel discussion at the University. The topic was "The American Work Ethic."

Paul: Sounds like that should have been a lively discussion.

Paulette: It really was. We started out by comparing an average American worker to their counterpart in other nations. Then, we addressed the question of declining American work ethic and closed the afternoon with a discussion on how America's entitlement approach to society contributes to the decline.

Paul: So, what were the major conclusions?

Paulette: Let's see...American immigrants are 30% more likely to start a business than non-immigrants. People from other nations work much harder and display greater work ethics to achieve the luxuries that Americans take for granted such as food, paved streets, running water and functioning sewage systems. American's entitlement mentality has worsened with time, to the point where much of America relies on things that have no perceived cost.

Paul: Wow...using an automobile as an analogy, it sounds like America's work ethic is in desperate need of new wheels.

Paulette: ...and a new engine, transmission, ignition system, lighting & signaling system, electrical system, doors, and windows.

YOUR POINT OF VIEW?

_____

_____

_____

_____

_____

_____

_____

_____

_____

_____

_____

_____

_____

_____

_____

_____

_____

_____

_____

_____

_____

_____

_____

_____

_____

About the Authors

Ervin (Earl) Cobb
Charlotte D. Grant-Cobb, PhD

The Cobbs are widely recognized as two of the nation's *rising-stars* among Self-Improvement, Relationships and Inspiration authors, lecturers and speakers.

The collective seriousness and wit of their work has been described as perfect for "those seeking personal growth, change and life enrichment but not quite ready for Dr. Phil."

Their prior books include *Until I Change, Living a Richer Life: Getting the Most out of Life's Gifts and Circumstances, Focused Leadership: A 10-Step Approach to Leading and Winning When it Matters, Transition* and *Navigating the Life Enrichment Model™.* Their newest video lecture series is titled, *Get Ready to Reap All the Richness Your Life Has to Offer.*

They currently reside in Phoenix, Arizona.

"Without consciousness and intelligence, the universe would lack meaning."

Clifford D. Simak

Bibliography

1. *Living a Richer Life: Getting the Most out of Life's Gifts and Circumstances* by Ervin (Earl) Cobb and Charlotte D. Grant-Cobb, PhD, Phoenix, Arizona: RICHER Publications, (2010).

2. *Driven: How Human Nature Shapes Our Choices* By Paul R. Lawrence and Nitin Nohria, San Francisco: Jossey-Bass (2002).

3. *Explaining Consciousness: The Hard Problem,* Edited by Jonathan Shear, The MIT Press, Cambridge, Massachusetts, London England, 1995-97, The Journal of Consciousness Studies.

4. *Power vs. Force: The Hidden Determinants of Human Behavior* by David R. Hawkins, Hay House Inc., Carlsbad, Ca. (1992, 1982, 2002).

"If you put yourself in a position where you have to stretch outside your comfort zone, then you are forced to expand your consciousness."

Les Brown

Index

Dialogues that Reflect the Average American's Thoughts and Suspicions

Index

Dialogues that Reflect the Average American's Thoughts and Suspicions

PILLOW TALK CONSCIOUSNESS

Intimate Reflections on America's 100 Most Interesting Thoughts and Suspicions

ALSO BY

ERVIN (EARL) COBB
AND
CHARLOTTE D. GRANT-COBB, PHD

BOOKS

Living a Richer Life
Getting the Most out of Life's Gifts and Circumstances

Focused Leadership
A 10-Step Approach to Leading and Winning When it Matters

Navigating the Life Enrichment Model™

Until I Change

Transition

VIDEO PROGRAMS

Get Ready to Reap All the Richness Your Life Has to Offer

All of the above are available at your local bookstore or may be ordered by visiting:

‡RICHER Publications
An Imprint of Richer Life, LLC

www.richerlifeassociates.com

www.ingramcontent.com/pod-product-compliance
Lightning Source LLC
Chambersburg PA
CBHW071144260626
47162CB00003B/914